MURDER AT BRAY MANOR

A HISTORICAL COSY MYSTERY

LEE STRAUSS

la plume
PRESS

MURDER AT BRAY MANOR
A Ginger Gold Mystery
Book 3
By Lee Strauss

Please note: British spelling is used in this book.

Series in order:
Murder on the SS Rosa
Murder at Hartigan House
Murder at Bray Manor
Murder at Feathers & Flair

Murder at Bray Manor

By Lee Strauss

Cover by Steven Novak Illustrations

Copyright © 2017

ISBN: 978-1-988677-05-7

*G*inger Gold folded the letter she was reading and dropped it on the side table. "Haley, do you believe in ghosts?"

Haley Higgins, an American student at the London School of Medicine for Women, lounged on the settee in the sitting room of Hartigan House as she sipped an after-dinner sherry. She arched a dark brow. "Why? Have you received mail from beyond?"

Ginger sighed as she put her feet up on the ottoman. She'd removed her strappy shoes but resisted the urge to unsnap her stockings and revert to bare legs. The lace border of her turquoise chiffon tunic draped casually over her knees. This recent frock acquisition from a well-known Parisian fashion house had thick embroidery along the bodice and a cluster of sequins that sparkled in the firelight.

Boss, her Boston terrier, curled up on her lap. She

petted his soft black fur. "It's a letter from Bray Manor —my sister-in-law, Felicia."

"Still unhappy about living in the country?" Haley asked.

"Frightfully. And I can't imagine Ambrosia moving from her family home. Even if Felicia was properly matched, Ambrosia would insist that the newlyweds lived there with her."

Haley clicked her tongue, commiserating. "Poor Felicia. How is the good Dowager Lady Gold anyway?

Ginger pushed locks of her red bob behind her ears, picked up the letter, and read.

Dearest Ginger,

I hope this letter finds you well. News of your new shop is exciting, and I'm very keen on visiting it one day—hopefully soon!

I'm writing to you because I'm concerned about Grandmama. Her nerves since we last visited you have grown worse, to the point where she now believes Bray Manor to be haunted. I haven't seen evidence of the supernatural, but Grandmama insists there is a poltergeist at work.

Oh Ginger, you promised to visit us and it's already been weeks! Could I prevail upon you to come speedily? I'm at a loss as to how to comfort Grandmama, and since you are so clever at solving mysteries, perhaps you can figure this one out, too.

With sincerest affection,

Felicia

"A poltergeist?" Haley said. A dark stray curl

escaped her faux bob and her lips pursed to the side of her mouth as she blew it off her cheek. "It sounds as if the elder Lady Gold is starting to lose her memory. It's quite probable that she moves things and forgets that she's done it. Her only conclusion is the interference of a mischievous apparition."

Ginger yawned, covering the chasm with the back of her hand. Since opening her new dress shop—Feathers & Flair—her days had been long, busy, and exhausting.

"You're probably right. Though, it's quite unfair of me to expect Felicia to bear the burden of caring for Ambrosia alone. Felicia's young and should be free to focus on her own life."

"You make a good point, Lady Gold."

Ginger had acquired her title through her marriage to the late Sir Daniel Livingston Gold, Felicia's brother and Ambrosia's grandson. He was buried in the family cemetery behind Bray Manor. Ginger had yet to visit his grave since her return to London, but something knotted in her chest at the thought of it. She wasn't quite yet ready to face the past.

Besides, a journey to Hertfordshire was the last thing Ginger needed at the moment. She had to fight against the irritation she felt at this new obligation.

"I just don't know how I can leave Feathers & Flair right now," she said. "It's still in its infancy and needs constant attention."

"Then don't go." Haley stretched, brushed down

her tweed skirt that hung mid-calf, and moved to the fireplace to stoke the flames. "Surely, you can employ someone to check in on Ambrosia for you?"

"I suppose. It just seems so heartless, and I did promise to visit before winter sets in."

"Then go."

Ginger cast a glance of annoyance at her friend. "Everything is so black and white with you."

Haley shrugged. "I'm a scientist."

Their conversation was interrupted by the sound of the telephone bell sound in the hall.

"Who could be ringing at this hour?" Ginger said.

Haley checked her wristwatch. "It's only nine o'clock."

"Really?" Ginger responded with another yawn. "It feels much later."

Pippins tapped on the door of the sitting room and stepped in. "Telephone for you, madam," he said. He was tall and slim with a bald head and skin sagging as it does when one is in his seventies. A loyal servant of the Hartigan family since Ginger was a child, she held the butler in high esteem and with much affection.

Ginger placed Boss on the floor. The dog stretched his hind legs then situated himself on the round Turkish rug in front of the fireplace and promptly went back to sleep.

"Who is it, Pips?" Ginger asked, using her pet name for him.

"Miss Felicia Gold, madam."

A pang of concern spread across Ginger's chest. First a letter and now a telephone call? She hurried to the hall and placed the receiver of the candlestick phone to her ear. "Felicia?"

"Oh, Ginger." Felicia's voice sounded thin and worried through the wire. "I'm afraid."

"Why? What's happened?"

"I thought Grandmama was losing her mind with her tales of moving objects, but now I've seen it for myself. The coat rack has moved, and I know Grandmama didn't do it because it's too heavy for her—and none of the servants admits moving it either."

"*Oh, mercy*," Ginger muttered. "Don't panic, Felicia. I'm sure there's a perfectly reasonable explanation."

"I don't mean to cause trouble, but would you come? Tonight?"

"Tonight? That's awfully short notice."

"Tomorrow then? Please, Ginger, I don't know what to do, and Grandmama is just beside herself with nerves."

"Very well," Ginger said, resigned. "I'll come tomorrow."

"Thank you, Ginger! I don't think I'll sleep a wink until you get here."

Haley sat upright when Ginger returned to the sitting room. "Is everything all right?"

"I don't suppose you'd like to join me on a short holiday to Hertfordshire."

"When?"

"Tomorrow."

"Oh, dear."

"Felicia is losing her head and I promised to come straightaway."

"It is soon the weekend," Haley said, "and as it happens, I don't have any classes tomorrow."

"So you'll come?"

"Only if we take the train."

"I'm not a bad driver!"

"I'm sorry, Ginger, you know I get ill when you drive, and I don't think I'll ever get used to traffic running on the left-hand side of the road."

"Fine," Ginger huffed, annoyed that Haley didn't trust her driving abilities. "We'll take the train." She was too exhausted to concentrate on the road for that long anyway. She might even be able to sleep a little on the way there. The rhythmic churning of the train wheels as the steam engine pushed on could make one quite drowsy.

Ginger patted her thigh and called to her pet. "Hey Bossy," she said as she scrubbed behind his pointy ears. "How would you like to go ghost hunting?"

CHAPTER 2

Ginger hurried down the wide staircase, circled from the second-floor where the bedrooms were to the marble floor of the entrance hall. Her newly painted fingernail trailed along the banister. She should have asked her maid, Lizzie, to wake her up earlier. As it was, she had dressed quickly in a white Habutai silk blouse, with its fashionable flat collar, tucked into a low-waist velour skirt with a hem at mid-calf. She usually wore something with more flair for the shop, but this outfit suited the train ride scheduled for later that morning. She had chosen a mushroom-shaped hat trimmed with black glycerine feather pompoms. Her shoes, black T-straps.

She nearly lost her footing on the emerald staircase runner and clung to the banister, preventing a turned ankle.

Lizzie, with Boss at her heels, had entered the hall in time to see Ginger slip.

"Are you all right, madam?"

"I'm fine." Ginger studied her nails, relieved to see she hadn't damaged her work. Lizzie usually painted them for her, but she'd been walking Boss—a new morning ritual.

Ginger smoothed out her skirt and turned on one heel to look behind her. "Are my seams straight?"

Lizzie drew closer, the nose on her youthful pixie face wrinkling as she squinted and examined the back of Ginger's legs.

"The right one's a bit crooked."

Ginger nodded, giving her maid permission to rectify the wayward hose. She hoped she hadn't forgotten to attach one of the garter straps in her hurry. She pressed a palm against the four points around her thigh until she was satisfied they were all properly fastened.

Lizzie went to work, and Ginger felt the maid's adept fingers pushing the seam until it ran up the centre of the back of the leg.

"There you are, madam."

"Thank you, Lizzie. You're a brick. Now can you do me a favour and pack a suitcase for me?"

"You're going away?"

"Just to Hertfordshire. I plan to catch the last train home tomorrow evening, but do be sure to include a little of everything, just in case. My Schiaparelli evening dress, the silver Vionnet, and my new Kate Reily."

"Yes, madam."

"And throw in several headbands. I've already packed my hats. The boxes are stacked by the dressing table." For such a short trip, Ginger would only take along a few hats. Hat boxes were cumbersome to travel with, especially when one wasn't taking one's own motorcar. Headbands did well in a pinch.

"Yes, madam," Lizzie said. Her eyes strayed to the dog sitting obediently at her side. "Will Boss be going with you?"

Ginger perceived the attachment that had grown between Lizzie and Boss over the last couple of months. "I'm sorry to separate the two of you," she said sincerely, "but it's only for a couple of days."

Ginger called for Boss to follow her into the kitchen. A trip to the countryside would be good for the dog and, though she was grateful to Lizzie for minding Boss, Ginger thought the time away would do to remind him that she was his mistress.

As usual, Madame Roux, the shop manager Ginger had employed for Feathers & Flair, was at the Regent Street store, preparing for opening. She always arrived first to turn on the lights and review the receipts from the previous day.

"Hello, Madame Roux," Ginger said warmly.

"Good morning, Lady Gold." Yvette Roux was a thin woman in her mid-fifties. She maintained a perfect posture and carried herself with grace and sophistication. Today, she wore a navy-blue French crepe dress with her black and silver hair partially covered in a matching velvet hat.

Feathers & Flair was bright and inviting with tall windows that let in natural light. The floors were polished white marble. The walls, creamy white. Electric crystal lamps hung from high ceilings that sported intricate mouldings painted gold. All the trimmings in the room were gold, a design choice Ginger had made to honour her family name.

The white brightness of the room was a perfect backdrop for displaying the latest in women's fashions. Ginger wanted to provide for those eager for a new frock immediately by supplying factory-made dresses. And for those willing to wait and pay for the service— she sold one-of-a-kind gowns.

Madame Roux hadn't been keen on a shop that sold both factory-made dresses and unique designer dresses. She felt it would confuse the customer. "Who is the client?" she questioned. "Society women or the middle class?"

Ginger had convinced her that, since the war, fewer women could afford personal fashion gowns, but still wanted the quality that many well-known designers were providing in factories. And the younger crowd actually craved the rack dresses, wanting the experience of choosing a dress and walking out in it in the same hour.

Ginger admired the dresses gracing the mannequins in the window. She found the jade Molyneux particularly pleasing and decided she must order one for herself.

"Is everything up to your expectations?" Madame Roux said. Her dark brown eyes grew bright as she gave Ginger her full attention.

"Yes, of course. Only, I'm afraid I'm needed in Hertfordshire for the weekend. I know it's sudden, and that the shop has just been open for a short while …"

Madame Roux laid a reassuring hand on Ginger's arm. "Do not worry, Lady Gold. I have years of experience running dress shops exactly like this one. It is why you employed me, no?"

Ginger smiled at the competent woman, her worry lessening to a certain degree. "Indeed, Madame Roux. I'll be back on Monday, so it's just for a couple of days. Hopefully, before the Paris order arrives."

"I'll look after that for you, Lady Gold, should you be detained."

Typically, Ginger would inventory the new product herself. She held in the sigh she felt building in her chest. This *was* why she employed Madame Roux. She should trust her to do her job.

"Perhaps you can swap a couple of the older dresses from the window. It's important to keep the showcase fresh."

"Yes, madam."

"When I return we can plan a Christmas sale."

"An excellent idea, madam."

Ginger double-checked the cash drawer, counted the float, straightened the scarves on a display rack, and ran a finger along the velvet hats to ensure they were dust free. She studied the stock in the back room where the extra dresses, hats, and accessories were stored. One corner was reserved for dress creation with a brand-new Singer sewing machine set up and ready to go.

Ginger walked the white floor tiles one more time taking everything in. Pride bloomed in her chest. She loved her shop and already felt a sense of anxiety at leaving it creep in.

"You go on," Madame Roux said. "The girls will be in shortly. Everything will be fine."

The "girls" were her three other employees: a seamstress, a fashion student at the Royal College of Art, and the floor clerk.

"I'll leave you the telephone number where I'll be staying," Ginger said. She found a pencil in the cashier drawer and scribbled on a small notepad. She pushed it over to Madame Roux. "In case you need me."

inger bought tickets for a private first-class compartment made from polished mahogany and lit with shiny brass lanterns. The seats were upholstered in olive-green though Ginger wouldn't have minded if the padding was a tad thicker.

Haley, comfortable in her customary tweed suit, sat across from Ginger, her nose tucked in a medical textbook. Boss was curled in a ball on Ginger's lap, snoring softly. The gentle rocking of the carriage had lulled the small dog to sleep in minutes.

Haley nibbled on the tip of a strand of curly dark hair which had escaped its faux bob, a bad habit Ginger had scolded her for on more than one occasion.

"Why don't you get your hair cut properly?" Ginger said.

Haley snorted. "With curls like this? It would be a nightmare to manage. I'd look like a chimney broom."

Ginger's gaze returned to the passing landscape before her, pastoral scenes of open fields dotted with farmhouses and small villages comprising of red brick houses.

The whistle blew, casting a billow of grey smoke across the moody autumn sky. Soon they would arrive. A wave of anxiety washed over Ginger and she placed her perfectly manicured fingers over her chest. Similar to when she had arrived at Hartigan House, Ginger braced herself to face the memories of her late husband, Daniel. The last time she'd visited Bray Manor, she'd been with him.

The train slowed as it chugged into the station.

"Bossy," she said as she clipped his leash onto his leather collar. "We're here."

The train came to a stop, and Haley snapped her book shut and stuffed it into her handbag.

"Interesting reading?" Ginger asked.

"ABO blood groups. Scientists are learning a lot about blood analysis now."

"That *is* interesting." Standing, Ginger smoothed out her autumn jacket, adjusted her hat and pushed one side of her short bob behind her ear.

Ginger hired a porter to remove the suitcases and hat boxes from the overhead racks. The doors to the platform opened and they stepped off into a small crowd of travellers, some going and some coming.

"I'll wave down a taxicab," Haley said, arm extended. A rickety black motorcar, at least a decade older than the taxicabs in London and barely more than a horse carriage on wheels, stopped in front with a skid and a wake of dust.

The porter and the driver each opened a rear door allowing Ginger and Haley to climb in and then tied up the luggage in the back. Ginger leaned forward and instructed, "Bray Manor, please."

The shock absorbers of the old taxicab were in need of repair, and the ride through Hertfordshire was bumpy. Ginger doubted the old thing even had inflatable tyres.

In the distance, cows and flocks of sheep dotted the low-lying hillsides. The darkening skies opened, wetting the road. Worn wipers scratched across the windscreen.

Eventually, they turned a corner, and Bray Manor came into view. The massive stone structure stretched out along green gardens. The rain darkened the red roof. Several chimneys belched smoke. The hooded attic windows bulged like watchful, sinister eyes.

Haley shivered. "I think I believe Ambrosia now."

"It's much less ominous looking in the summer," Ginger said.

The taxicab driver parked near the entrance. Ginger paid him and then, with Boss in her arms, hurried out of the rain to the front door and rang the bell. A five-tone chime could be heard, and the wooden door soon opened to a serious-faced bald-headed butler on the other side.

Ginger didn't recognise the man. He was new since she'd been here last.

"Hello, I'm Lady Gold. Dowager Lady Gold is expecting me."

"Of course, madam," the butler said. "Do come in."

A damp Haley followed, rain dripping from her hat brim. The butler's lips twitched in barely concealed disapproval.

Bray Manor was vast, making Hartigan House feel like a doll's house in comparison. Felicia's voice echoed as she crossed over to her new guests.

"Oh, Ginger, you made it! I'm so glad you're here!"

Felicia Gold was what the rags called a "bright young thing." Just twenty-one, her skin was porcelain-smooth, and her straight-cut chiffon dress shimmered with the kind of energy that Ginger missed. Felicia had a teardrop-shaped face with eyes that reminded Ginger of Daniel, without, of course, the dramatic eye shadow and mascara Felicia wore.

Ginger embraced her sister-in-law. "It's good to be here."

"And Boss came, too," Felicia said, patting the dog on the top of his small head. "Perhaps *you* can sniff out our poltergeist." Boss let out an agreeable whimper and licked the top of Felicia's hand.

Felicia turned to Haley. "Nice to see you again, Miss Higgins. So good of you to come."

"It's a pleasure," Haley replied.

Turning to her butler, Felicia instructed, "Wilson, do take Lady Gold and Miss Higgins' things to their rooms."

Wilson began hauling Haley's suitcase and Ginger's bags upstairs. A second trip would be necessary, perhaps even a third.

"Grandmama is in the drawing room," Felicia said, waving for them to follow her. "She's just dying to tell you all about the ghost."

"Do you actually think Bray Manor is haunted, Felicia?" Ginger asked.

"Logically, no. But this old place is so dreary, especially when the weather is poor. The way the wind whistles through the windows, it's easy to let the imagination go wild."

The drawing room was lost in the Victorian era. Thick curtains framed tall windows, a lush Turkish carpet—immediately claimed by Boss—sat on the wooden floor in front of an elaborately designed fireplace. Plush furniture with smooth, curving wood trim encircled a long oval tea table. Wallpaper, in a green and gold geometric design was covered, ceiling to floor, with framed paintings of various sizes. It hadn't changed in ten years.

As if Ginger had stepped into the past, Daniel was there, sitting in the chair with the pincushion back, the legs of his well-pressed suit crossed languidly, a pipe gripped with one confident hand. Ginger remembered that they had dressed for a hoity-toity event with the Duke and Duchess of Berkhamstead, and how Daniel's jaw had grown slack when she entered, his eyes glistening with pleasure as he took her in.

"Mrs. Georgia Gold, the most beautiful of women."

Ginger had smiled at the use of her new legal name. She'd shed Georgia Hartigan that summer of 1913 when they wed. Ginger was a pet name given to her by her mother.

"Oh, Georgia. Thank goodness you're here."

Ginger snapped back to the present. An elderly white-haired woman in a high-collared blouse and a brown, floor-length velvet skirt, sat on the edge of a green, velour high-back chair. Her brass-top walking stick was propped up beside her. She wrung a white lace handkerchief between wrinkly, aged-spotted hands. Ambrosia often reverted to the use of Ginger's Christian name when she was wound up.

"Hello, Grandmother," Ginger said.

The older woman didn't waste a moment for pleasantries. "I just can't bear it any longer. Not only are strangers continually underfoot, now this. A poltergeist! I'm barely mistress of my own home!"

Ginger and Haley sat on the settee.

"Oh, hello Miss Higgins," Ambrosia said as an afterthought. She didn't share Ginger's enthusiasm in bringing the lower classes into their confidences, especially *foreigners*.

"Hello, Lady Gold."

Felicia rang the bell and ordered tea.

"Strangers underfoot?" Ginger asked. "What do you mean by that?"

"I'll explain," Felicia said as she sat in the vacant chair next to her grandmother. "As you know, Bray Manor has been under considerable financial difficulties." Felicia kept her gaze averted at these words. Everyone in the room knew that Hartigan money had been keeping Bray Manor afloat since Ginger married Daniel. And Ginger had been reticent to pour more of her inheritance into what appeared to be a perpetual money pit.

"Well," Felicia continued with a smile, this time locking her gaze on Ginger, "I came up with a plan. Bray Manor is a large dwelling with many unused rooms—why not rent them out? A short advertisement in the local paper produced many takers. In fact we now have three associations that meet regularly; the knitters' circle, the stamp collectors, and a gardeners' association."

Ginger was impressed with Felicia's ingenuity. "What an ingenious idea," she said.

Ambrosia knocked her walking stick on the floor. "It is *not* an ingenious idea. It's sordid and dreadfully humiliating. If we're that hard up, we should just let the place out and move elsewhere."

"Grandmama," Felicia said with a tinge of impatience. Ginger had no doubt the two of them had discussed this topic ad nauseam. "We've tried that. No one wants a big house like this."

Ambrosia snorted and stared out of the window. "Still, I can barely raise my head in public. It's like living in a museum with strangers plodding along, staring, and making comment. On *my* things."

"We're no longer in Victorian times, Grandmama," Felicia said, her tone haughty. "We live in the modern world now. Scandals are perfectly screaming."

Ambrosia huffed. Ginger found it interesting that Ambrosia had let Felicia go ahead with her plans. As the matriarch, she could've stopped her granddaughter if she really wanted to. Ginger grinned. The dowager always liked to put on a good show.

"Next we'll be letting out Livingston Lake," Ambrosia muttered. "Every Tom, Dick and Harry cluttering the jetty."

Haley followed Ambrosia's gaze. "Jetty as in a dock? Is there a lake nearby?"

Ginger motioned to the long narrow windows. "There's a rather large pond out the back."

Ambrosia twittered. "It's a small *lake*. Bray Manor does not have a *pond*."

Ginger smirked at Haley. "My mistake. There is a rather small *lake* out the back."

Haley strolled to the closest window and peered outside. "I see. How fortunate."

"Renting out the lake is a splendid idea, Grandmama," Felicia said with a mischievous twinkle in her eye. "That would be one way to get the men together. I could invite my single female friends over and we could 'fish' for husbands."

"Such cheek!" Ambrosia said. "See what I put up with, Georgia? An insolent child *and* strangers in my home."

"Come now, Grandmama," Felicia said. "You find it convenient, too." To Ginger and Haley she explained, "Grandmama is a member of the knitting circle. They meet here at Bray Manor."

Ambrosia harrumphed. "One has to do something to keep occupied. Besides the parish hall is damp and draughty. My joints ache when I'm there, and quite frankly, I don't enjoy the smell."

The maid returned with a tea tray in hand and placed it on the elegantly engraved sideboard. Starting with Ambrosia, she delivered cups of tea one by one. She then put a plate of biscuits on the low table the women encircled before leaving them once again.

Ginger sipped her tea and placed the cup on its matching saucer. "So tell me about this ghost, Grandmother."

"It's quite dreadful," Ambrosia said. Her teacup rattled against the saucer. "My nerves are shattered."

"Things . . ." Felicia hesitated. "Small things began to go missing."

"Theft?" Haley asked.

"I thought so at first, but then the items would turn up again, but in places where they don't belong. Like flower arrangements in the cloakroom. Framed pictures off the wall and on the floor. The staff are quite flustered."

Ginger frowned. "It sounds to me as if one of them is having fun at your expense."

"They wouldn't!" Ambrosia insisted. "My servants are loyal."

Felicia nodded. "I tend to agree with Grandmama. I just can't imagine any one of them stooping to do such a frightful prank."

"Any new staff members since you started renting rooms out?" Ginger asked.

"That would quite defeat the purpose of earning money," Ambrosia said, sitting stiff in her chair. "The staff is capable of cleaning one or two extra rooms."

"What about Wilson?" Ginger asked. "How long has he been with you?"

"Wilson's been the butler here for six years," Felicia said. "Our previous butler fell ill."

"When did the 'poltergeist' start to manifest?" Haley asked. "Would it be around the time the associations began meeting here?"

"There is a corresponding coincidence," Felicia said.

"Does the ghost strike on the same day of the week?" Ginger asked.

"No, that's the strange thing," Felicia said. "I made a note of it, myself. I wondered if a member of one of the associations was involved, but it seemed to happen on any given day."

"I'd like to see the membership lists," Ginger said.

"I thought you would." Felicia walked to the sideboard, opened the top middle drawer and removed a file. "This has the names and addresses of all association members meeting at Bray Manor and telephone numbers for those who have a telephone."

Ginger accepted the file. "I'll take a look at this later. When is the next association meeting?"

"Tonight," Felicia said. "The knitters' club. They meet every Friday."

"And the other associations?" Ginger asked.

"The stamp collectors on Tuesdays. The gardeners on Wednesdays. Oh, and, this is so exciting!" Felicia shook her shoulders and smiled with enthusiasm. "We are hosting a charity dance tomorrow night, here at Bray Manor. You'll still be here for it, won't you?"

"A dance?"

"It's to raise money for the Croft Convalescent Home," Felicia's eyes sparkled. "To help those poor soldiers who've returned to Hertfordshire with grave handicaps. Give them a leg up and that sort of thing."

"We were going to catch the evening train,"

Ginger said. "I have my shop, and Haley has her studies."

"Oh, too bad," Felicia said slyly. "I've been walking out with someone. I thought it would be fun to introduce you."

"Walking out?" Ginger said. "With a gentleman?"

"Of course."

"Perhaps we can meet him earlier?" Ginger said.

"Oh no," Felicia said with a glint in her eye. "If you want to meet him, you'll have to come to the dance."

"Grandmother," Ginger said. "Do you know who your granddaughter is talking about?"

"No," Ambrosia said, her expression sour. "The child won't tell me. Young people these days are simply outrageous. I'd never have dreamed of behaving in such a disrespectful manner in my day."

"Well," Ginger said, her curiosity piqued. "I do love to dance. And it does sound like a great cause, doesn't it Haley?"

CHAPTER 4

The maid, Phyllis, led Ginger and Haley up the grand staircase to the bedrooms on the second floor. Ginger took the room at the very end of the hall—Daniel's former room—and Haley two rooms down next to the lavatory.

Electric light hadn't been introduced to the upper floors, and Phyllis lit the candle before leaving Ginger alone. While Ginger usually found candlelight to be comforting, the evening had yet to grow dark, and the flickering flame beating against the twilight that reached inside created a sense of gloom.

It didn't help that the last time she'd slept in the large king-size bed, framed in dark mahogany with four tall decorative bed posts, Daniel had been alive. She wrapped her arms around her stomach, trying to picture crawling into that massive bed alone.

The window slammed shut with a bang, extinguishing the candle. Ginger nearly jumped out of her skin.

Ginger's mind went to the improbable. *Ambrosia's poltergeist?*

She felt her way through the darkness to the dressing table where the candleholder lay, her fingers fumbling over the smooth surface until they found the box of matches. She adeptly struck one and relit the wick. The shadow of a man with a gun appeared along the far wall, and Ginger dropped to the floor, an instinctive defensive manoeuvre. She almost called out to him when she noticed a toy soldier sitting on the dressing table beside the candle. The inanimate décor was responsible for the shadow and for the falling of Ginger's heart to her feet.

Feeling silly, Ginger was thankful no one had been around to witness her fear.

Scanning the room in search of a second candle, Ginger let out a small breath of relief when she spotted a short one on the bedside table. She quickly lit it, her eyes searching the room, reassuring herself that she was indeed alone.

When Ginger checked the other windows, she found them all to be shut and locked. The maid must've opened one to air the room out and the wind had drawn it closed. No wonder Ambrosia was frightened, her imagination taking flight. This old house could scare a ghost.

The knitting circle met in the sitting room, the only association to do so. The others met in a rarely used nondescript room in the opposite wing. When questioned Ambrosia muttered, "If I'm going to attend an association in my own home, I might as well be comfortable."

The walls of the sitting room were stained a rich, dark brown, and a deep burgundy rug was situated on the wooden floor in front of a stone fireplace, now glowing orange with flames. Boss made himself at home on the carpet in front.

The members sat in a semi-circle around the fireplace, and with Felicia, Ginger, and Haley present, they totalled eight.

"Ladies," Ambrosia began, "this is my late Daniel's wife, Lady Gold and her friend Miss Higgins. You know my granddaughter Miss Gold." To Felicia, she added, "So nice of you to join us tonight, child."

Greetings were extended from around the circle. "To your right Ginger, is Mrs. Richards, she lost her husband in the war." Mrs. Richards was a plump woman with short tight curls peeking out from under a flat hat. Her eyes were exceedingly small, peering out behind gold-rimmed spectacles. She inclined her head toward Ginger with a tight smile.

"Beside her is Miss Smith. She volunteers at the Chesterton Library." Miss Smith looked to be in her late thirties, well into her spinsterhood, an unfortunate situation now as with so many younger women competing for so few men. She grinned while shrugging narrow shoulders and finger-waved. "How do you do?" She had a soft voice and spectacles that balanced on the tip of an upturned nose.

"Miss Whitton," Ambrosia continued, "works as a nurse at the Croft Convalescent Home, and last but not least," she said with a lazy flick of her heavily jewelled hand, "the Honourable Mrs. Croft." To explain the title for Haley's benefit she added, "Mrs. Croft's father-in-law is Baron Julius Croft."

Miss Whitton reminded Ginger of a younger version of Haley, possessing the same mass of dark curls—only hers were cut short in an actual bob—and a no-nonsense aura. The Honourable Mrs. Croft had a manly sort of appearance with broader shoulders than hips, and large hands, however her full bosom was unmistakably feminine.

Tea was served by Phyllis, the parlour maid, clad in a black uniform skirt and white apron, and hat. Immediately the knitting needles were drawn.

"Mrs. Saxton's daughter is having twins," Miss Smith said. She raised her needles to present a half-finished baby boot.

"Are we to knit baby things?" Ginger asked.

"Not at all," Ambrosia said. "Some of us are knitting blankets for the convalescent home, some of us winter socks, hats, and scarves for the poor and homeless, and some for our own selves.

Ginger noted the look of disappointment Ambrosia flashed at Mrs. Richards.

Mrs. Richards noticed it, too. "I'm not knitting for myself, thank you very much. This is for my daughter." She held up a lemon-yellow cardigan. "She needs every bit of help she can get to find a husband with so many of our young men gone."

"There are never enough wool blankets," Miss Whitton said, displaying the grey mass draped over her legs. "Winter's coming, and our war veterans don't deserve to be cold."

"I'm knitting this for my Patrick," the Honourable Mrs. Croft offered. She held up a forest-green jumper. It brings out the green—"

"Oh for pity's sake," Ambrosia sputtered. "Don't say in his *eye*. We all know he lost one in the war."

The Honourable Mrs. Croft scowled at the dowager. Felicia failed to hold in a giggle, and Ginger thought it a good time to jump in. "I think I'll stick to knitting a scarf for the poor." She was good at many things, but knitting was not one. Even a simple, long rectangular creation was a challenge. The lines narrowed when they shouldn't. At least the flaws weren't noticeable when the finished project was wrapped around the neck. She thought no one suffering in the cold would mind. "How about you, Miss Higgins?" she asked to keep the conversation civil.

Haley displayed a near-finished hat. "It helps if

you actually knit while you talk," she said to Ginger's obvious look of dismay.

Ginger worked her needles together, *knit, purl, knit, purl*. When she'd managed a couple of rows, she said, "Mrs. Croft, I take it the convalescent home was started by your family?"

"Yes," Mrs. Croft replied, a look of pride flashing behind her eyes. "When my son returned home, terribly disfigured, I knew there were other damaged soldiers whose families couldn't care for their physical and emotional well-being like we could with our Patrick." She added with forced humility. "It seemed the right thing to do."

"A generous response to the needy," Ginger said.

"Accolades are perpetually in short supply," Ambrosia uttered in a near-whisper, her eyes never leaving her handiwork. Mrs. Croft pierced her with a glare.

No love lost there, Ginger thought.

"I understand there is to be a benefit dance hosted here at Bray Manor tomorrow evening," Ginger said in another effort to diffuse the obvious tension between the two women.

Mrs. Croft's eyes lit up. "I dare say, there is. Please do say you plan to attend."

"As a matter of fact, Miss Higgins and I shall both be there."

Felicia squealed, her eyes betraying her excitement.

Mrs. Croft pushed on. "Marvellous. I can't wait to introduce you to Patrick."

Ginger addressed the room. "Will everyone be attending?"

"Only because I support the cause," Mrs. Richards said.

"I'll come," Miss Smith murmured. "Though I'm not likely to dance."

"Why not?" Ginger asked.

Miss Smith looked up over her glasses. "I'm not usually asked."

"Nor am I," Haley said sympathetically. "We can be wallflowers together."

"Oh, stop that nonsense," Ambrosia said. "The men are crippled. They'll hardly be picky."

A corporate gasp quieted the room. Felicia's hand flew to her mouth as she stared incredulously at her grandmother.

Ambrosia, feeling the disapproval of her fellow knitters, quickly added, "I don't mean to be harsh, but that *is* the reality."

"Dowager Lady Gold," Mrs. Richards said, adeptly changing the subject, yet with a twinkle in her eye. "Are you still being troubled by your *ghost*?"

"You laugh," Ambrosia said as if on guard. "But there *is* a poltergeist living in Bray Manor. Just yesterday, I left the book I was reading on that occasional table over there, and this morning, a maid found it in the ground floor lavatory."

"Is it possible that you carried it there yourself, and simply forgot about it?" Miss Whitton asked.

Ambrosia dropped her knitting. "Most certainly not! I would never visit the *ground floor* lavatory."

Miss Smith tittered.

"I'll ask you what you find so amusing, Miss Smith?" Ambrosia said.

"Oh, nothing Lady Gold." Miss Smith's cheeks warmed to rosy. "I was just reminded that I need to use the ground floor lavatory, myself."

Ginger and Haley watched the diminutive librarian leave the room and then shared a look. Had the poltergeist just shown her hand?

Felicia made several glances at her wristwatch.

"Do you have another appointment?" Ginger asked, her smile playful.

Felicia's shoulders slumped. "I'm afraid I find knitting rather dull."

"What's that on the end of your needles?" Ginger asked. Felicia worked with needles nearly the diameter of her little finger. Large needles produced large stitches which made knitting things like scarves and blankets go much faster. Ginger had used the technique often herself. She pointed to the large, shiny pink dots on the ends.

Felicia paused her domestic duty and admired her knitting tools. "So boring to work with plain wooden rods. I thought a touch of my new nail polish would make them more interesting."

Ginger laughed at her playful sister-in-law.

Attuning herself back to the group conversation, Ginger caught the last bit of Miss Smith's question to Ambrosia.

". . . The archery association is looking for a new place to meet. There's a nice patch of lawn at the front of Bray Ma—"

Ambrosia held up a heavily lined palm. "Let me stop you right there, Miss Smith. I've had quite enough of the local populace traipsing about my home."

The knitting circle adjourned promptly at nine. Felicia almost sprung to her feet, leaving her knitting basket behind as she hurried away. Wilson accompanied the members to the entrance hall after the obligatory farewells. Ambrosia called on her maid, Langley, and took herself to bed. Ginger and Haley were left alone to enjoy the final embers glowing from the fireplace.

"Miss Smith is a funny little thing, isn't she?" Haley said.

"Grandmother was quite hard on her," Ginger said. "I fancy Miss Smith isn't keen on being spoken down to like that."

"Who would?"

"Do you think she's striking out at Grandmother with trickery? Grandmother can be overbearing and domineering, especially to those she feels are stationed beneath her."

Haley huffed. "I'm aware. I'm surprised she's lowered herself to join the knitting circle."

"The war has levelled out the classes somewhat," Ginger said. "I'm sure having the Honourable Mrs. Croft in the association plays a small part."

"How so?"

"If the Honourable Mrs. Croft can lower herself to knit with the lower class, then the Dowager Lady Gold must as well."

"Complicated business, this class system of yours."

"You're telling me."

Ginger removed three sheets of notepaper from her handbag. "These are the member names from all the associations. Miss Smith is also part of the Stamp Collectors Association which met yesterday, but so is Mrs. Richards."

"Either of them could be our poltergeist, then," Haley said.

"Except that doesn't answer for the wayward candelabra from the dining room that ended up hiding in here on the floor behind the globe. That happened on Wednesday."

"What association meets on Wednesday?"

"The Gardening Association. Miss Whitton and Mrs. Croft."

Haley shook her head, "It's a mystery."

Ready to call it a night, Ginger gathered her shawl and knitting basket. "So kind of Felicia to set us up with supplies." Her eyes landed on Felicia's knitting basket left behind on the floor. "Oh, oh."

"What is it?" Haley asked.

Ginger picked up the ball of wool and the unfinished afghan her sister-in-law was working on. "It looks like our poltergeist has struck again. One of Felicia's knitting needles is missing."

CHAPTER 5

"This is getting ridiculous," Ginger said. "Do you recall which staff members have come through the sitting room in the last hour?"

"Phyllis collected the dirty dishes," Haley said.

"Wilson followed the ladies out of the room," Ginger added. "You and I were already seated and facing the fireplace. He would've had a chance to slip it up his sleeve."

"Ambrosia rang for her lady's maid."

"That's right. Evelyn Langley assisted her upstairs. As much as grandmother hates to admit it, she doesn't like to do the stairs, at least not at night when the lighting is dim."

"Langley carried Ambrosia's knitting basket for her. She could have easily collected Felicia's knitting needle and tossed it into Ambrosia's basket."

Ginger hummed. "A mystery, indeed."

As much as Ginger hated to interfere with what went on below stairs, she was desperate to get to the bottom of the matter. Ambrosia would cling to her until she did so, and she did need to get back to London. "I think it prudent for me to question the staff in the morning," she said.

Later Ginger ran into Felicia in the upstairs passage and told her about the poltergeist's latest sleight of hand.

"These silly games are so juvenile," Felicia said.

Ginger agreed. "Indeed. Tell me more about the staff."

"Phyllis is the parlour maid, but also helps in the kitchen."

"Are the others also performing double duty?"

"Wilson is both butler and chauffeur, and Evelyn Langley attends to both Grandmama and me. She helps Mrs. Beasley, our cook, and Phyllis when she's not needed by one of us."

It wasn't uncommon since the war for big houses to scale down on staff and require more from the ones kept on. At Hartigan House, Ginger was guilty of it herself.

However, the staff themselves wouldn't be pleased with this new way. Disgruntlement could lead to practical joking—a seemingly harmless way to blow off steam. Perhaps the entire staff was in on it together?

The next morning Ginger stepped through the green baize door to the servant's area. Unlike the rooms occupied by family members or guests, the servant side was dimly lit with oil lamps, and several candles were in use. Ginger made her way to the kitchen where many of the staff were busy with various tasks.

The vast kitchen had a grand cast-iron stove with a brick, wood-burning oven. High-set windows faced the wooded area, letting in natural light, while an electric lamp added to the room's brightness. A massive wooden table filled the centre of the flagstone floor.

Mrs. Beasley was almost as wide as she was tall, with a round face and stubby arms. She was busy stuffing the carcass of a headless goose. Short dark hair poked out from under her white cap, and her full cheeks were rosy from her exertion.

"Langley, put the lemon tarts in the oven," Mrs. Beasley ordered. "Wilson, I think we need more wood. Phyllis, you can roll out the pastry for the goose pies. It's in the cold pantry."

"I wish I were going to the dance," Phyllis said. "It sounds so exciting."

"Stop your daydreaming," Mrs. Beasley said. "You'll be needed for cleaning up afterwards."

Phyllis pouted, and abruptly turned her back on the cook. She shuddered to a stop when she noticed Ginger standing in the doorway, and nearly dropped her bowl of potatoes. "Milady," she said, her voice jumping an octave. Wilson, Langley and Mrs. Beasley turned to face her. The women dipped and Wilson bowed.

"I'm sorry to disturb you, and on such a busy day, so I'll be quick. Miss Gold has had a personal item go missing. Lately, as you know, Bray Manor has been victim to petty trickery and unlawful handling of items belonging to both Miss Gold and the Dowager Lady Gold.

"What a terrible matter that is," Mrs. Beasley said. "We will all keep our eyes peeled."

Each one, with their eyes to the floor, nodded.

Mrs. Beasley couldn't possibly have taken Felicia's knitting needle, but the others all had the opportunity. Ginger couldn't accuse any of them without proof. She hoped a personal talking to would correct the aberrative behaviour.

"I do hope you'll do your bit to stop the culprit," Ginger said. "Please do find me if you have something you need to get off your chest."

Ginger left the kitchen feeling as if she had just made a wrong move. Servants had so little to call their own, it felt brash to march into what they considered their domain.

But no, she had every right to enter the servants' area. Bray Manor might not be her house, but it was her late husband's house and the home of close family members.

She found Haley and Ambrosia in the sitting room.

Ambrosia was as ruffled as a hen having her eggs stolen from underneath her.

"I feel simply invaded," she huffed as she grasped at the high collar of her blouse. "Strangers in the garden, walking on the lawn, traipsing through the house, doing whatever they like with no word to me at all. I can't believe I let Felicia talk me into this. The associations are bad enough, but now a ball?"

Ginger helped herself to a cup of tea from the hot pot sitting on the sideboard. "Grandmother, it's for a good cause. And it'll be cleaned up tomorrow, you won't even be able to tell it happened at all."

"I do hope you're right. Although, a good deed such as this might divert the wagging tongues from our other humiliation."

"You mean the fact that you're renting out rooms."

"Yes, of course. What else could I mean?" Ambrosia leaned forward on her walking stick and said to Haley, "Would you mind getting me some tea?"

Haley smiled and spoke softly to Ginger as she approached the sideboard. "I'd die for a strong cup of coffee right now."

"I'm afraid Ambrosia believes the brew is evil, but I'm sure I can have a pot mustered up for you if you like."

"I can manage without it for now. Tomorrow morning would be much appreciated, though."

Ginger sat casually across from the fire and adjusted her rayon day dress, the colour of ripe plums. Her eyes landed on Felicia's knitting basket and frowned at the single needle. Ambrosia followed her gaze and gasped.

"Felicia's knitting needle? Has the poltergeist taken *that*, too? Where do you suppose it shall show up now? The kitchen? The study? My rose garden? Ginger, I simply can't take this anymore. You must do something!"

Ginger worried the elderly woman would succumb to the vapours. Haley hurried over with the requested tea.

"Are the missing items always found on the ground floor?" Ginger asked.

Ambrosia stilled. "Yes, I suppose that's true."

Haley muttered, "A poltergeist who knows its place."

Felicia blew in, her youthful face aglow. "Isn't this all so intoxicating?! It's been ages since we've had so much life at Bray Manor. I've invited my best female friends. We're all eager to dance with the brave soldiers tonight." She smiled softly Ginger's way. "Some of them were childhood friends of Daniel's."

Ginger's lips felt dry but she resisted moving her tongue over them. She swallowed, curious on why Felicia's mention of Daniel stirred up complicated feelings. She'd talked of Daniel often over the years,

Haley knew all about him, but being here at Bray Manor, it was like picking at an old wound.

"I look forward to meeting them," Ginger replied.

Ambrosia put her weight against the brass knob of her walking stick and stood. Ginger moved to help her up, but Ambrosia waved her away. "I'm quite capable of getting out of a chair."

She strutted out of the room and the atmosphere, sparking like lightning, followed her. Haley let out a long windy breath and Ginger laughed. Felicia dropped into an empty seat and crossed her legs, kicking out the top one and swinging it up and down like a water pump.

"You're a bundle of nerves," Ginger said to her.

"I'm just excited."

"Her *friend* is coming," Haley said slyly.

"That's right," Ginger said as if she'd forgotten. "Now that you've trapped us here for the dance, will you tell us about him?"

Felicia's leg pumped harder then came to a full stop. She did a partial turn in her seat and leaned forward. "I won't tell you his name, except for this, he's a captain in the army."

Haley whistled. "A captain. Impressive."

"He's so fetching," Felicia gushed. "I can't believe he's interested in someone like me."

"What do you mean?" Ginger said. "You're a catch in every way. Beautiful, intelligent . . ."

"But not titled or monied," Felicia said, her enthusiasm waning. "Only the appearance of it."

"Does it matter?" Haley asked, indignant.

"Money always matters," Felicia said matter-of-factly. She sprung to her feet. "I'm going to get ready. I've been waiting for this moment for *ages*."

"I suppose we should get ready, too," Ginger said, suddenly not feeling like going to a dance party.

"Do you have a dress?" Haley said. "I didn't pack for dancing. Not that I have anything for such an event anyway. I'll just spend the night in my room, reading."

"You can't do that. You promised Miss Smith you'd be a wallflower with her!"

"Right, I did."

"I brought an extra dress you can borrow."

"I thought you didn't know about the dance."

"I didn't. I always pack for every possible occasion."

Every occasion. Ginger's eyes were drawn to the motion outside the window and her gaze focused on the far side of the lake where the cemetery lay. She'd packed a black dress.

Haley followed her gaze and asked gently. "Are you going to visit it today?"

"No," she answered. "Maybe tomorrow." Her heart pounded as she imagined her husband's gravestone. Actually seeing it would make everything too real.

Daniel's death. Her guilt.

CHAPTER 6

The ballroom at Bray Manor was transformed. The crystal chandeliers glimmered, casting a starry array of warm light. Candelabras flickered on the ends of the refreshment table, which provided water and punch. Dancers were sure to work up a thirst. In the corner, for those searching for something stronger, a drinks trolley was parked. Yellow ribbons looped along the walls with a huge banner reading: Remembering our war veterans.

A six-piece band with its sweet strings and warm horns in three-four time played *Dreamy Melody*, enticing dancers to waltz around the hardwood floor.

Ginger and Haley arrived together and stood near the drinks trolley where they each accepted a flute of champagne. Ginger wore her Kate Reily evening dress—a pale green silk satin with a brocaded floral and vine design, a colour Ginger knew brought out the green in her eyes. It was trimmed with a delicate lace at the neckline and cuffs, and the wide satin sash's metal tassels drew the eye.

Haley fussed with her borrowed Madeleine Vionnet, a lovely sleeveless, creamy frock, with elaborate pearl beading on the bodice and generous layers of handkerchief-hemmed skirting. Its classic bias cut created soft lines that hung gracefully over Haley's thin frame.

They both wore long white gloves that reached their elbows, and Ginger linked their arms together.

"I feel so odd," Haley said. "Like I'm pretending to be someone else."

Ginger nudged her playfully. "Then pretend to be someone having fun."

Ginger observed the room, noting the number of wounded men. Interspersed were the non-military folk there to show their support by dancing and hopefully emptying their pockets. The soldiers here were lucky—or someone would say, unlucky—to have made it home. They sat or stood awkwardly along walls, some staring blankly into the twilight out of the windows. Had her Daniel lived, he would be amongst them.

Most noticeable were the men in wheelchairs and on crutches. Others were missing arms, wearing eye patches, or even partial facial masks to cover burns and missing facial features. The soldier talking tersely to the Honourable Mrs. Croft—presumably her son, Private Patrick Croft—was one of them.

Even after five years of peace, the sight of these men and knowing what they'd sacrificed, scorched a hole in Ginger's stomach.

"A dance seems like an odd choice of event for these men," Haley said.

"Dancing is a delightful gift. Why should they miss out?"

"You make a good point. So, who asks whom in this situation?"

The matter was settled when two soldiers approached, one on crutches who asked Haley to dance, and one with a missing left forearm, who stretched out his good right hand to Ginger.

"You don't mind?" he said. "I can't hold your waist, which is a deuced shame, believe me."

Ginger laughed. "Not at all." She gripped the soldier's shoulder with one gloved hand and held his palm with the other. She caught Haley's eye as her friend became her dance partner's crutch, and they swayed awkwardly to the music as they shared an amused grin.

Ginger's partner talked nervously, relaying his regiment and his tours of service, and where he had been wounded.

"Did you know Sir Daniel Gold?" she asked.

"I did. A fine lad. We were chums as children. He never had airs, you know. Treated us all like his equal.

Insisted that we called him Danny, and that stuffy titles were for pretentious old men." The soldier laughed at the memory, then quieted. "Did you know him?"

Ginger stared up at the young man, feeling stunned. She'd just assumed he would know who she was, but then why would he? There were no formal introductions at this dance as it wasn't a society event.

"He was my late husband," she said, her words soft.

The soldier froze. "You're Lady Gold?"

"I am."

"I—I'm so sorry," he stuttered. His ruddy face flushed knowing that he was dancing with one above his station. "Had I known . . ."

"You wouldn't have asked?"

"Yes, madam, I mean, no, my lady . . ."

"Then I'm glad you didn't know."

The music ended and Ginger thanked the soldier for the dance. "Please don't tell your mates who I am. It would distress me terribly if I never had another offer to dance again tonight."

Ginger spotted Felicia at the refreshment table and called out to her. She didn't respond, and Ginger concluded the music had drowned out her voice. She tapped on her sister-in-law's shoulder only to be stunned when the woman who turned failed to be Felicia.

"I'm sorry," Ginger said. "I thought you were someone else."

"How fun," the young woman said. "Who?"

"My sister-in-law, Felicia Gold. You have a very similar profile."

"Oh, you must be the much-spoken-of Lady Gold!" She held out her hand. "I'm Angela Ashton, a friend of Felicia's. How do you do?"

"It's a pleasure," Ginger said.

"Ginger!" Felicia joined them along with another girl, all dressed in straight-cut silk-over-rayon dresses, with thin straps and billowy hemlines. They sported similar hairstyles cut short with shiny finger waves and wore beaded headbands sprouting large feathers.

"I see you've met Miss Ashton. This is Miss Webb," Felicia said referring to the mousy brunette.

"We should all ask the wheelchair men to dance!" Miss Ashton said. "Wouldn't that be a hoot?"

"But how would that work?" Miss Webb asked. "They're in chairs."

Miss Ashton giggled mischievously. "You sit on their laps, silly!"

A gloved hand went to Miss Webb's ruby-red lips. "How frightfully scandalous!" she said with a glimmer in her eye. That said, she was ready to play. "Let's do it!"

Felicia laughed and shot Ginger a faux look of apology. Ginger laughed back.

Ambrosia scuttled to Ginger's side, her walking

stick *click, click, clicking* on the wooden floor. Her round eyes widened further with disbelief as the daring girls pushed wheelchair-bound soldiers to the middle of the floor and hopped on their laps. The men seemed all too eager to spin them around.

"My word!" Ambrosia stated. "What on earth has got into those girls' heads?!"

"They want all the soldiers to feel included, Grandmother. The dance is for their benefit after all."

"But it's so unbecoming! And look at that saucy Miss Ashton. She's engaged, you know, to Mr. Croft."

Ginger was surprised at this announcement. "Really?"

"One of those impulsive measures that was so common among the young before the war," Ambrosia explained. "But when poor Mr. Croft returned home damaged, her enthusiasm wavered greatly."

"How sad for Mr. Croft," Ginger said. "But why not break off the engagement, if that's the case?"

"He says it's a matter of honour, much to the Honourable Mrs. Croft's chagrin, I can tell you. Miss Ashton is after a title, plain and simple. Mr. Croft will inherit his grandfather's barony soon. Mr. Croft's father, sadly, has passed away, and poor Sir Julius Croft is now on his death bed."

"I'm sorry to hear that," Ginger said lowering her gaze. "But, surely after so long, Mr. Croft needn't go through with it. No one would judge either of them."

"Tell that to Miss Ashton. She's determined to

hold him to it. And just look at her giggling and flirting with that soldier like a trollop!" The soft folds of skin on Ambrosia's face flushed red with indignation. "Mrs. Croft has done her absolute best to keep the nuptials postponed. She's hoping in time, she'll change her son's mind and defy the hold Miss Ashton has on him."

Ginger studied Patrick Croft as he watched his fiancée, her bare arms draped around another man's neck, spinning in circles, her head back in giddy laughter. His mouth was turned down in a firm scowl, and even though he had only one eye, it was narrowed and piercing.

"Miss Ashton might be doing the Honourable's work for her," Ginger said.

The song ended, and the wheelchaired men, with countenances noticeably cheered, were pushed back to their friends by their dance partners, who were immediately asked to dance again by fellow soldiers.

Only Felicia refused, her eyes set on the entrance. Ginger followed Felicia's gaze to the uniformed man who stood, hat in hand and with an air of self-importance. She gasped.

"*Oh, mercy.*"

CHAPTER 7

*F*elicia pranced across the room and practically threw herself into the man's arms. He pushed her back with a look of restraint, and she, with a flash of hurt in her eyes, restrained herself. Instead, they shared a demure cheek-to-cheek kiss.

Felicia's offence was short-lived and she dragged the soldier over to Ginger and proclaimed proudly, "Ginger, this is Captain Smithwick. Captain, my sister-in-law, Lady Gold."

Captain Smithwick stood tall, shoulders back and stared at Ginger with a glint in his eye. "We've met," he said. "Nice to see you again," he added with a smirk, "*Lady* Gold."

Ginger's blood iced at the sight of the man—a person she'd hoped she'd never have reason to see again in her life—and now her heart stirred with a renewed swirl of anger and contempt. "Captain Smithwick," she said coldly.

Felicia, in her blush of new love, failed to register the animosity.

"I'm so glad you made it, love," she said. "I was worried for a while."

"I said I'd come, and I'm a man of my word."

Ginger scoffed, then politely turned it into a cough, covering her mouth with her gloved hand.

"Are you all right?" Felicia asked.

"Oh, yes. Just, I think I need a drink. Excuse me."

Ginger immediately found a waiter and helped herself to a glass of champagne. Smithwick's arrogance! His cold-heartedness! There was no doubt that he knew Ginger would be here. What did he want with her now? And how dare he use Felicia and her tender emotions to get to her!

A wall of French windows faced the back, and dancers regularly slipped outside to cool off or to smoke cigarettes. Ginger strutted to the nearest one, passing Angela Ashton on her way. Miss Ashton was angled away from her and spoke sharply to her friend Miss Webb.

"Don't be such a limp squid, Muriel. Honestly, I don't know why Felicia invited you. You have no mind of your own."

Muriel pouted and stormed out of the hall.

Ginger frowned. Miss Ashton certainly wasn't in her best form.

Outside, the wind was brisk and cool, soothing the heat of anger ignited by Smithwick. Ginger tightened her shawl over her shoulders and breathed deeply. She wouldn't let that man get to her.

The lights from the dance lit the patio, but beyond, in this moonless night, was blackness. Only the soft lapping of the waves whispered of Livingston Lake in the distance.

Ginger had barely got her emotions under control when she sensed someone behind her. She turned to find Mr. Croft.

"Lady Gold," he said with a nod. The red tip of his lit cigarette arced through the darkness as his hand moved to his lips and he inhaled.

"Hello, Mr. Croft," Ginger said. "Are you having a good time?"

Mr. Croft dropped the butt of his cigarette and stubbed it out with his toe. "I would be if you'd give me the honour of this dance."

Ginger smiled and accepted his outstretched hand. "I'd be delighted." They entered the hall just as the band began to play Isham Jones's upbeat *Who's Sorry Now*.

Ginger focused her attention on the soldier's good eye. Once she got past the horrible scarring on the left side of his face, she found that the uninjured half was quite pleasant. Before the burns, Mr. Croft had been a handsome man. The scarring must've continued down the left side including his hand, as he wore a lone glove to cover it.

Mr. Croft proved to be a good dancer, expertly leading her through the quickstep.

"Are you enjoying the evening?" Mr. Croft asked politely.

"Oh, yes. It's quite fun. I do hope the Croft Convalescent Home will do well."

"We are very appreciative of the Gold family for your support."

Over the soldier's shoulder, Ginger saw Miss Smith, the petite volunteer librarian from the knitting circle, dancing with the same one-armed man Ginger had danced with earlier. Miss Smith was a wallflower no more.

Mr. Croft wasn't much for talking, but he turned out to be a good dancer, and Ginger found she could lose herself in the movement and simply enjoy the jazz number. She found herself singing along. "Who's sad and blue? Who's crying too? Just like I cried over you. Right to the end . . ."

"You have a pretty voice," Mr. Croft said.

"*Oh mercy*, I'd forgotten myself!"

"Don't be embarrassed. I quite liked it."

Ginger tilted her head up and smiled. She couldn't help but feel annoyed at the shallowness of Miss Angela Ashton. Mr. Croft was a gentleman.

As they continued to circle the room smoothly Mr. Croft stumbled slightly before quickly recovering.

Ginger saw the reason for her partner's distraction. Captain Smithwick and Miss Ashton were having a row. Not loud enough to break through the sound of the band, but it was quite obvious by the look on their faces.

Miss Ashton at it again.

Smithwick grasped the girl by the wrist. Ginger scowled. The captain loved to exert control over those he considered weak.

"Excuse me," Mr. Croft said, breaking away from Ginger. He swiftly crossed the dance floor to interfere in the altercation. Ginger worried it might come to blows, but the sight of Mr. Croft, soon-to-be Baron Croft, was enough to prompt Smithwick to loosen his hold. Mr. Croft took Angela's hand in his and pulled her onto the dance floor, preserving to a measure, her dubious reputation.

Ginger joined Haley at a table and sat with relief. "Dancing is so hard on one's feet," she said.

"Only if you dance non-stop, my friend."

Felicia was now on the dance floor with Smithwick and Ginger glowered.

Haley followed Ginger's line of sight her gaze latching onto the waltzing couple. "You don't like the captain, do you?"

"No."

"Wow. Not even a stab at social niceties to soften the blow. Care to explain?"

Like all matters of the war, Ginger had vowed

silence, and her dealings with Captain Smithwick were no different.

"I just don't trust him."

"That much is clear."

Haley was used to Ginger's secretiveness when it came to the years before they met, and she let the matter drop.

The song ended, and Felicia and Smithwick joined them. Ginger forced herself to smile and feign politeness.

"How long are you in town, Captain?" Ginger asked.

"I'm stationed in St. Albans," he said.

"We met at a dance club there," Felicia said. "Miss Ashton, Miss Webb and I go once in a while to break the awful monotony of Chesterton."

"I see."

"Ginger," Felicia said, frowning. "Is something wrong?"

"Not at all, darling," Ginger lied. "I'm just knack-ered. I think I'll retire early."

"Please do honour me with a dance before you go," Smithwick said. He stared at her in a way that suggested she'd do better to say yes. Ginger didn't want to further stir Felicia's suspicions, and besides, she was curious.

"Of course, Captain."

They swirled around the room to *God be with our Boys Tonight*, which had been a hit during the last year of the war. The emotion that registered on the faces of the soldiers as they remembered those dark times —sadness, remorse, trauma—made the back of Ginger's throat sting. She pinched her eyelids closed to keep the threatening tears at bay. Dancing with Captain Smithwick reminded her of a similar instance in France when they'd waltzed together to this very song. Ginger worked hard to keep the memories buried away, and she resented Captain Smithwick for blatantly disturbing them.

"What is it that you want from me?" she finally asked.

"I want you to come back."

"Into service? Whatever for? The war is over."

"You seriously can't be that naive?"

"Why? Do you think otherwise?"

"I fear the peace we fought for will elude us."

"Oh please, don't say that."

"It's true, my lady. Stresemann's government is tenuous at best. The German mark is now ten billion to one pound. *Ten billion*. I can't say much at this moment, but I can tell you that Prime Minister Baldwin is very concerned."

Ginger knew Smithwick's words were true. And in another life, the one where Daniel was alive and she was a warrior, she would be eager to step up to fight. In *this* life, she didn't think so highly of herself to believe the world would live or die based on whether she agreed to join Smithwick's team again or not. She had family to take care of now. She was all Ambrosia and Felicia had left.

"I'm sorry. You'll have to look for someone else."

Captain Smithwick wasn't the type to give up easily. "Surely you must be bored to tears after years of great adventure." At one time Ginger longed for the challenge of travel and intrigue, but Daniel's death had put an end to such passions. Everything changed for her on that cold September day.

"I've recently opened a dress shop."

Smithwick scoffed. "A *dress shop*? You must be joking."

Ginger felt offended by the captain's belittling tone. "I've done my duty for king and country and now I plan to live my life on my terms. I'm out."

Ginger pulled away, but the captain held firmly and tugged her back to his chest.

"Why do you despise me so?"

"You know why."

"Because of *La Plume*?"

"You didn't have to do it."

"That was my jurisdiction now, wasn't it? Not yours."

"Innocent people died."

"That's the sad consequence of war."

Ginger scowled—the bitterness of her distaste for the man thick on her tongue. "Now that you've found me and heard my answer, you can let Felicia go."

Smithwick grinned facetiously. "Why would I do that?"

"Because your feelings for her are insincere, a mere ruse to get to me."

"It stings that you think so little of me. I could've found you another way."

"Why didn't you?"

"Because I thought your concern for Felicia would sway your answer."

"I will not be blackmailed! And if a hair on Felicia's head…"

"Calm down. Felicia is safe. Though I'm sure she'll hate you for pushing me away and breaking her heart. Especially after I ask for her hand in marriage, then blame you for breaking it off."

"You're despicable."

"I've been called worse. I say, why don't you take a night to think about it."

"No need. Good evening, Captain."

Felicia met Ginger at the door with fire in her eyes. "Is there something going on between you two?"

"Of course not. What do you mean?"

"You looked like you were having a *lovers'* spat! Did Daniel know?"

"Know what? Wait, no! Smithwick and I are *not* involved." Not intimately anyway.

"You can have your choice of any man, Ginger, with your money and your looks and your title. Just keep away from mine!"

Felicia disappeared in a wind of fury. Ginger ran after her but in the dimly lit passage, missed seeing what direction Felicia went. She searched the manor, Felicia's bedroom, the library, telephone room, and sitting room, even outside on the patio, but her sister-in-law refused to be found.

CHAPTER 8

*G*inger, with Boss at her heels, met up with Haley in the morning room early the next day. Mrs. Beasley had fashioned a nice spread of bacon and eggs, kippers and tomatoes, fried sausages, and buttery toast, despite the extra work the dance had created for her.

"Felicia's not down?" she asked.

"Not yet, but you know how that girl can sleep," Haley said.

Ginger poured a cup of coffee from the vacuum flask. "How's the coffee?"

Haley shrugged. "Weak, but we're in England so what else is new. At least an effort was made to make it."

Ginger settled into her chair and sighed.

"Hard night?" Haley asked. "You look tired."

LEE STRAUSS

"I didn't sleep well. I'm afraid Felicia and I had a terrible row last night."

Haley stared out over her coffee mug. "I can't imagine over what."

"Captain Smithwick."

"Oh. Yes, I *can* imagine. But do go on."

"She fancies herself in love and sees me as a threat."

Haley arched a dark brow. "Are you?"

"Hardly. I can't stand the man."

"Hate is the opposite side of the coin to love."

Ginger cut a small piece of sausage and held it low beside her chair, allowing Boss to gobble it up.

"Well, in this case, both sides are hate."

"I'm sorely curious as to what the man did to deserve your wrath."

"It hardly matters now. I just wish he'd leave Felicia alone."

"Maybe he truly cares for her."

Ginger almost spat out her tea. "He doesn't. The man only cares about himself. He just used her to get to me."

"What does he want from you?"

One of the many things Ginger disliked about secret service was all the *secrets*. It felt like she constantly had to lie or tell half-truths. After a while, it got hard to differentiate real life from playing a part. It wasn't her nature to be dishonest.

"Like I said, it doesn't matter now. I'm not budging, and he'll tire of Felicia. I'm just sorry the poor girl is going to get her heart shredded."

Haley nibbled on a piece of bacon. "Who among womankind hasn't? It's a rite of passage."

Boss scampered to the window and barked.

"What is it, Boss?" Ginger said. She stared out of the French windows toward the lake which was nearly invisible in the early morning haze. A man suddenly materialised, his face broad with the look of horror as he stumbled across the lawn.

"It's the gardener," Ginger said as she jumped to her feet. "He's in distress!"

Haley followed Ginger as she raced out of the glass doors.

"Clement?" Ginger called out. "Is something wrong?"

"Oh, Milady! It's horrible!"

"Are you in pain?" Haley asked. "I'm a nurse."

"Not me, miss. Over there."

Ginger strained to see through the haze. What was the gardener pointing at? Dark fur? An animal? Something lay at the water's edge. Boss, ears erect and stubby tail vibrating, barked a warning.

"It's a g-girl, madam," the man sputtered.

A girl? With dark hair? Ginger's heart grew heavy with dread as she sprinted to the form. "Felicia!"

Part way out of the water, the body lay face down. The party dress floated up by the knees, a dirty feather drooped from her headband. "Felicia!"

Ginger fell to the earth and reached for the arm—icy cold and clammy to the touch—she pulled the body over. The once pretty face was thick with bloat, the flawless skin a transparent, ghostly blue. Makeup smudged blackly around soulless eyes.

Ginger's breathing hitched.

Not Felicia.

The dead woman was Angela Ashton.

Ginger closed her eyes in relief, feeling shame at the gratitude she felt.

"Ginger," Haley said gently. "You shouldn't touch the body." To the gardener she said, "Go to the house and ask Wilson to call the police."

Haley squatted beside Ginger. "You thought it was Felicia."

Ginger rolled the body back to the position she'd found it in and rubbed the stress lines that had formed between her brows. "Yes, for a moment, I did."

"Do you believe Felicia's life is in danger?"

Ginger considered the question, then shook her head. "No. I was mistaken."

"Miss Ashton did have a lot to drink at the dance," Haley said. "Maybe she wandered too close to the lake and fell in." Haley scanned the body and frowned. "Wait a minute. Look at this."

A rose-coloured stain had blossomed on the left side of the corpse's back.

"What is it?"

Haley carefully pulled the fabric away from

the skin.

"A puncture mark."

"From what?" Ginger asked.

"I don't know."

Wilson, his long face as sombre as a headstone, arrived with the news that the police had been summoned. "Shall I get you your coats?" he asked. "And umbrellas? It's beginning to spit."

Ginger only just noticed the goose pimples on her arms. "That would be perfect, Wilson, thank you. And if you see Felicia, try to keep her inside."

"Yes, madam."

"Do you really think the butler can keep Felicia from doing what she wants?" Haley said.

Ginger sighed. "You're right, I know. It was unfair of me to ask."

Wilson returned with umbrellas, opened each one and offered them to Ginger and Haley. "The police have just arrived, madam," he said. Behind the butler, two black-uniformed officers strutted towards the scene. Ginger approached them.

"Hello. I'm Lady Gold, the granddaughter of the Dowager Lady Gold, and this is Miss Higgins. We're visiting Bray Manor for the weekend. This . . ." she motioned to the body, legs still immersed in the pond, "is simply dreadful."

"Indeed, madam," the older officer said. "The name's Sergeant Maskell, and this here is Constable Ryan." Both officers squatted low for a closer look.

"Do you know who she is?" the sergeant asked.

"Her name is Angela Ashton. She was a guest at the benefit dance last night. A friend of my sister-in-law."

"Right, t'ball for t'Croft Convalescent Home," Constable Ryan said with an Irish lilt to his voice. "I planned to go to dat, but I had to work in t'end." He cast a disapproving glance at Sergeant Maskell.

"We couldn't all be at the dance, now could we?" the sergeant responded defensively. "You were outranked by your seniors, plain and simple." He shrugged at Ginger. "I'm not one for dances myself."

"Members of the local police were at the dance?" Ginger asked.

"We're not a big lot," the sergeant explained. "Only four of us. Dicky and Harry jumped at the chance to dance with a lot of pretty lasses."

"Even dough Dicky is married and had to bring his wife," Constable Ryan said with a note of disgust. "I, at least, am single."

"Officers," Ginger said, pointing to the body.

"Yes, right," Sergeant Maskell said. "I take it the girl had been drinking and stumbled into the lake? That kind of thing happens at parties with girls who can't hold their liquor."

"An accident, den," Constable Ryan stated.

"I'm not so sure of that," Haley said, her expression alternating from amusement to disdain. "There is a puncture wound here, on her left side."

"She fell into the reeds," Sergeant Maskell said.

"In that case, there would be more than a single wound," Haley countered.

"Or fell into something she was holding in her hand," Sergeant Maskell countered back.

Haley turned to Ginger. "We should call the medical examiner."

"The medical examiner?" Sergeant Maskell asked. He latched fat thumbs into his belt loops and rolled on his heels. "Dr. Guthrie's not interested in random deaths, miss. He's quite crotchety about that. He'll examine the body once it's taken to the surgery."

"This may not be a 'random' death," Sergeant," Ginger said.

The officer's eyes widened in understanding. "Are you suggesting this is . . . murder?"

"We can't discount it at this point," Haley replied.

"B-but," Constable Ryan, stuttered, "we've never had a m-murder in deese parts, not since I can remember."

Sergeant Maskell blew a raspberry through thick lips and shook his head. "Blimey."

Haley made the request to Wilson and twenty minutes later the medical examiner arrived.

"Dr. Guthrie!" Sergeant Maskell puffed out his chest, and then declared, "It appears we have a murder."

CHAPTER 9

*T*he medical examiner, a tall man with stooped shoulders and a wild mass of white hair that hadn't seen a comb in a while, pushed past the police offers with long strides and grunted, "Make way!"

When the man squatted, his pointy knees jutted out to the side, and Ginger couldn't help but compare him to a gigantic grasshopper.

Ginger made introductions to which Dr. Guthrie merely grunted again. "Miss Higgins is a student at the London School of Medicine for Women."

For the first time, Dr. Guthrie took a moment to assess Haley who squatted beside him. He hummed, pulling in his lips—it was hard to determine if he was impressed or bothered.

"There is an entry wound, but no exit wound," the doctor said as he flipped the body from front to back. "She might've been shot." He stood, joints creaking as he straightened. "I'll search for the bullet when I perform the post mortem." He stared at the sergeant and spoke as one would to a child or a new employee. "Do make sure to take plenty of photos before the body is moved, include every angle, and then have the remains delivered to me." With that he strutted across the lawn towards the house.

"Cheery fellow," Haley muttered, then jogged after him. "Might I assist you, Doctor?"

Without glancing back at her, Dr. Guthrie grunted again. "If you must."

Haley called out to Ginger. "I'll telephone when I need to be picked up."

"Madam," Constable Ryan said as he approached Ginger, his lips pulling up sheepishly. "Lady Gold, might we trouble you for a camera? I'm afraid dere isn't one at t'Chesterton station."

Ginger felt her eyelids flutter at the admission. Bray Manor appeared to be frozen in time. "I'm sure there's one around," she said, then called to Wilson who'd since returned from the telephone room and asked him to enquire.

"Ginger?"

The finger waves of Felicia's bob were flattened on one side and the make-up not removed from the night before, smudged around her eyes. She wore a simple cotton day dress and a wool cardigan with low-heeled strapless shoes. "What on earth is going on?"

Her gaze then landed on the body at the edge of the lake. Her complexion drained of colour as she gripped the buttons of her jumper. "Oh, dear Lord."

Picking up the hem of her dress she sprinted, nearly slipping on the dew. Ginger caught her arm in time, sparing her a nasty fall.

"Steady, Felicia," Ginger said.

"Who is it?" Felicia said, panting.

"It's Miss Ashton."

"Oh, no!" Felicia pulled away from Ginger's grip. "Angela!"

Constable Ryan hurried to block her path. "You mustn't touch t'body, miss."

Felicia's knees gave out and she folded. Her watery grey eyes demanded an explanation. "What happened to her? Did she fall off the jetty? Did she drown?"

Ginger held her tightly and spoke, keeping her voice steady. "We can't be sure. The medical examiner wants to do a post mortem."

Ginger gently pushed dark flyaway hair off Felicia's face. The vulnerability in her sister-in-law's eyes smote her. "Let's go inside." Her voice was gentle. "You're wet and shivering."

"Yes." Felicia's voice sounded thin and fragile. She allowed herself to be guided to the sitting room where Ginger sat her in front of the fire and then rang the bell for some tea.

A folded knitted rug lay across the back of the

settee, and Ginger draped it over Felicia's pale body before claiming the next chair nearest the fire.

After the tea was delivered, Felicia said, "It's my fault."

Ginger looked up over her teacup. "That can't possibly be true. Why would you say such a thing?"

"I should've made sure she got home safely, saw that she got into a taxicab. She was my friend. I should've known that she'd gone outside to the lake. Instead . . ." She glanced at Ginger with eyes of regret. "I was sulking over the silly quarrel I had with you."

Ginger reached over and patted Felicia's hand. "This is not your fault. Miss Ashton was a grown woman, not a child in your care. Miss Webb got home fine without your help."

Besides, there were others around who could've watched over her, but Ginger didn't say this aloud. People like her fiancé Mr. Croft, and the aforementioned Miss Webb.

Or Captain Smithwick.

Wilson entered the room and announced Sergeant Maskell and Constable Ryan.

The two officers stood before the women, helmets in hand, casting sideways glances at each other. Neither appeared comfortable with their unenviable task.

Wilson had located a Brownie camera, which Constable Ryan held under one arm. "We'll have to keep dis for the time being," he said. "Until t'negatives are developed."

Ginger nodded. "Of course."

"Ghastly business," Sergeant Maskell said. "Simply ghastly."

"Is there something else that you need?" Ginger asked

Sergeant Maskell gruffly cleared his throat. "We'll need to run a proper investigation. Unfortunately, this requires us to intrude on your privacy and trespass on your goodwill. We should like to interview everyone in the house who was here last night."

"I completely understand," Ginger said. "Would you like to begin with us?"

Sergeant Maskell and Constable Ryan shared another look. "If you don't mind, madam," the sergeant said. "We'll be quick about it."

"Do proceed," Ginger said. "But keep in mind that Miss Gold has just suffered a shock. Miss Ashton was one of her dear friends."

"We'll make this as painless as possible," Sergeant Maskell said. "Miss Gold, how long have you known Miss Ashton?"

"We served together as land girls towards the end of the war. Being middle-class and older, Angela, Muriel, and Jean had worked there for some time before I showed up. I was underage, but looked old enough, I guess, since the officials believed me when I lied. I don't think they were picky by that point anymore, and I just couldn't stand doing nothing while Daniel was daily risking his life. You can only imagine how livid Grandmama was, but I was determined to do my bit. Knowing I could be as stubborn as she was, Grandmama finally relented, but insisted that I came home every night."

Felicia sipped her tea, then returned the cup to its saucer with a trembling hand. "We worked on a farm, caring for sheep. The girls were grateful for the extra set of hands; they didn't care about my society status. Everyone was too tired to worry about such nonsense." She dabbed a tear from her eye. "Angela was always so courageous. Rounded up those big sheep for shearing, like a pro. I confess, the beasts frighten me. But I'm competitive by nature, and I wouldn't let fear get in the way of my keeping up with her."

"Who is Jean?" Ginger asked. This was the first time the name had come up.

"Jean Smith," Felicia's gaze locked onto her hands cupped together on her lap. "She . . . died."

Had the poor girl succumbed to the flu pandemic of 1918? As if the death count from the war wasn't enough to bear, many souls had gone on from this earth as victims of the disease. Before she had a chance to ask, the sergeant spoke again.

"Did Miss Ashton, uh, have any, uh, gentlemen friends?"

Ginger's chin shot up. "She was engaged to Mr.

Croft. I'm sure that's common knowledge in these parts, isn't it Felicia?"

"Well, yes, I would think so. They've been engaged for ages."

Sergeant Maskell swallowed. "The grandson of Baron Croft?"

Felicia nodded. "The one and only."

Sergeant Maskell spoke to Constable Ryan out of the side of his mouth. "We need to interview the Crofts."

"Right, sir."

"Jot that down."

Constable Ryan stuffed a hand into his pocket and retrieved a small notebook. "Yes, sir."

"Where would I find the Dowager Lady Gold?" Sergeant Maskell asked.

"She attends church on Sunday mornings," Felicia explained. "Normally, I attend with her, but she excused me this once in light of the dance and how late it ended."

Ginger had wondered why Ambrosia hadn't materialised. The woman couldn't stand it when she wasn't in the centre of excitement. As if summoned by the poltergeist itself, the tap, tap, tap of Ambrosia's walking stick on the hard wood of the entrance hall announced her arrival.

She entered the sitting room with her feathers ruffled. "That motorcar! Old as the hills and slower than black treacle."

Bray Manor had one motorcar, a 1904 Coventry Humber. Ginger didn't doubt Ambrosia's assessment of its performance. Molasses did probably move faster. Perhaps she should donate her Daimler. It was only five years newer, but the mechanical advancement in automobiles during that period of time had been outstanding. Ginger thought she'd like to buy a new motorcar one day, anyway.

Ambrosia collapsed in her chair with a huff. "Constantly stuttering and backfiring—my poor heart nearly gave out. I half expected to be shot in the back."

Felicia glanced at Ginger in mortification. It was possible that someone *had* been shot in the back.

Ambrosia rang the bell for tea, aggressively, as if that would relieve her agitation. "It makes one miss the horses," she said. "Despite their awful smell. A horse never broke down on the way to church."

Having let off steam, the older woman finally noticed the police in the room. Her eyes darted to Ginger.

"What are they doing here?"

The sergeant made quick introductions. "I'm Sergeant Maskell, madam, and this here is Constable Ryan."

"Grandmother," Ginger said. "There's been a terrible discovery down at the lake."

Ginger paused and Ambrosia snorted with impatience. "Do go on!"

"A body's been found."

Ambrosia's eyes bulged at the news. "You've got to be joking."

"Sadly, no, Grandmother. It's Felicia's friend, Miss Ashton. She was discovered this morning by Clement. It's all very shocking."

"I'm afraid, madam," Sergeant Maskell began, "that we'll have to intrude on your privacy as we proceed with our investigation."

Ambrosia flopped against the back of the chair as if in a faint. "What next? The circus comes to town and occupies Bray Manor?"

"Grandmama!" Felicia cried with accusation. "How can you be so insensitive?"

"Me, insensitive? *I* didn't die on someone else's property."

Felicia tightened the rug around her shoulders and left the room in a huff.

"I can hardly keep up with the emotional ups and downs of that child," Ambrosia said after a beat. "We are all far too dramatic."

Sergeant Maskell and Constable Ryan observed the interaction between the three Gold women like creatures under a spell.

Phyllis arrived with the tea and Ginger brought a teacup to Ambrosia. "Drink this, Grandmother. It'll settle your nerves."

Ambrosia shook a crooked finger in the air. "Bray

Manor is haunted! Didn't I tell you, Ginger? The poltergeist has gone too far this time!"

Sergeant Maskell raised a bushy brow. "The poltergeist?"

Ginger hurried to explain. "Things have been going missing lately."

"Not missing," Ambrosia stated with exasperation. "Moved!"

The sergeant and constable shared a look. Like almost everyone else, Ginger perceived they believed the poltergeist to be a figment of an old woman's imagination.

Not Ginger. She believed her grandmother. The poltergeist existed. Though where Ambrosia thought it was an apparition, Ginger was certain the ghost was one hundred percent flesh and blood.

Wilson entered the room and declared, "Telephone for you, Lady Gold. Miss Higgins is on the line."

"Officers," Ginger said, not wanting to tip her hand that the call would contain news that should go to the local police first. "Please be seated. I'll return shortly."

Ambrosia didn't take to sitting alone with strangers, even lawmen, and rang the bell for her maid.

Ginger took the call in the telephone room. After relaying her message Haley asked, "Can someone pick me up? Or should I catch a taxicab?"

"I'll come for you straightaway."

"Ginger . . ."

"It'll give us a chance to talk in private." Ginger rang off before Haley could protest further.

Helmets in hand, the officers stood when Ginger returned to the sitting room. Langley hovered behind Ambrosia and Ginger excused her even though the poor girl had just arrived. She announced her news once the maid had gone.

"Sergeant Maskell, I'm certain a call has gone into the station from Dr. Guthrie. That was my friend Miss Higgins. She's a medical student and had accompanied Dr. Guthrie back to the surgery where a post mortem was performed. Miss Ashton did not die of a gunshot wound."

"That's good, then, innit?" Constable Ryan said, his face relaxing in relief. "She drowned in an accident."

"I'm afraid not," Ginger said. "Miss Ashton was dead before she hit the water. I'm afraid it's most certainly a murder."

Both men slowly lowered themselves back into the chairs, expressions slack with uncertainty.

Oh mercy, Ginger thought. These fellows are in over their heads.

"May I offer a suggestion?" she asked

"By all means," Sergeant Maskell said.

"Call Scotland Yard for assistance. Ask for Chief Inspector Basil Reed. Tell him I told you to call.

CHAPTER 10

*W*ilson was reluctant to hand over the keys to the Humber. "Are you sure you wouldn't like me to drive you, madam?"

"And where would we put Miss Higgins? There's only room for two on the bench."

"Miss Gold sits on the dickey seat at the back."

Ginger released a soft snort. Haley was nervous enough about motorcar travel in England. Ginger could hardly imagine her deposited in the back like a piece of luggage.

"I'd prefer to drive it myself."

Wilson's long nose inched upwards as he handed the key over. "It's not so easy to drive as the new model motorcars. The process is rather . . . involved."

Ginger gripped the key tightly. She'd had plenty of opportunities to drive old vehicles during the war, but she needn't defend herself to Ambrosia's butler. "Thank you, Wilson."

The Humber was parked in an outhouse specifically built to shelter the motorcar. Ginger took a moment to admire the old thing. A little rusty, it had been well driven over the years. Ginger understood the butler's attachment.

The olive-green exterior had two small doors that opened to a single, brown leather bench. Flat black wings scooped up over narrow tyres. Big lamps, like protruding bug eyes, flanked a diamond-shaped grille.

Recollecting the steps needed to start these old automobiles, Ginger wondered if she'd been too quick to dismiss the butler.

While standing outside of the vehicle she pulled the choke, located near the right front bumper. Then she hurried to the front of the motorcar, turned the crank beneath the radiator a quarter-turn clockwise to prime the carburetor. Jumping back inside, she inserted the key into the ignition and turned it. To set the idle, she pushed the timing stalk up and moved the throttle stalk down. Pulling the handbrake back, she placed the motorcar into neutral.

Ginger then jumped back out of the motorcar and turned the hand crank a half-turn, hoping the engine would start. She let out a breath when it sputtered to life. She brushed the dust off her coat, a deep burgundy ankle-length wool garment with a wide fur-trimmed collar and a large single button that fastened at the hip. She wished she'd taken the time to change into proper driving clothes.

Once on the road, the little automobile motored along proudly. Just as she reached the outskirts of Chesterton the Humber backfired, a shotgun noise that had Ginger braking and ducking. Reflexes from the war. Her heart hammered in her chest as she poked her head up to peek over the dash and through the broad windscreen. Another motorcar slowed up beside her, a new model Bentley.

The driver called out to her. "Everything all right, madam?"

Ginger adjusted her broad-brimmed hat and pasted on a smile. "Forgive me," she said. "My motorcar is a temperamental old thing. I'm fine now." She put the Humber into gear, and waved a gloved hand. The man tipped his hat and motored off.

Chesterton was a quaint English village with wandering lanes and brick houses claimed by ivy and wisteria vines. Two-level brick or stone businesses lined the main street with the usual amenities: post office, grocer, ironmonger, chemist, tobacconist, and a public house or two. The Chesterton Inn at the end of the road loomed larger with three floors and twice the width.

The surgery was on a windy lane off the main street, and thankfully Felicia's instructions were easy to follow. Ginger pulled up to the kerb. Haley spotted her from inside the entrance doors and met her in the street.

"Where's the horse?" she said facetiously.

"This beauty is barely a step up," Ginger said with a grin. She patted the bench beside her. "Hop in."

The swollen clouds over Chesterton decided now would be a good time to let go of their watery load. Fat drops dotted Ginger's shoulders. Ginger jumped out to release the hatch of the canopy. "Get the other side," she instructed Haley.

Together they drew the canopy over the seat and hopped in for cover.

"Such an adventure and we haven't even started driving," Haley said dryly.

Ginger worried the Humber would choose this inopportune time to break down, but happily, she was proved wrong, despite several sputters and backfires.

Haley wasn't as believing and hung tightly to the door handle. "At least this thing won't buck us off," she said stiffly. "Will it?"

"We're fine," Ginger said with a light smile. "What was it like, working with Dr. Grumpy?"

Haley chuckled. "He *is* a prickly old thing. Makes me appreciate Dr. Watts even more." She glanced at Ginger. "Are you returning to London with me tonight?"

"I can't. I'm worried about Felicia." Ginger

relayed the story of Felicia seeing Angela Ashton's body and falling into a state of shock.

"Poor girl," Haley said. "I remember the first time I saw a dead body. I had nightmares for days, and it wasn't even someone I knew well."

Ginger's mind flickered to her first dead body. Bodies, rather. Bloody war.

"I think the most Sergeant Maskell and Constable Ryan have had to deal with is disputing farmers or perhaps the odd traffic incident. They both grew pale and lost the will to stand when I presented the situation as a murder."

"Oh dear," Haley said.

"Thankfully they were happy to heed my suggestion to call Scotland Yard."

Haley's brow jumped and Ginger pretended not to see it.

"Does that mean the debonair inspector will be visiting?"

Ginger lifted a shoulder. "They could send anyone. How would I know?"

Haley hummed in a way that Ginger found exasperating.

"Even if Inspector Reed should be sent, it doesn't —" Her voice cut off as the motorcar dipped sharply in and out of a pothole.

Haley shouted. "Watch where you're going!"

"I am!"

Bray Manor beckoned from a distance and

Ginger let the topic go. She didn't know why Haley's light teasing got under her skin.

Basil Reed was nothing more than a friend to her. Not even that.

Not really.

CHAPTER 11

They found Mrs. Beasley resting with her feet up in the staff dining room, a plain rectangular space with white walls. A large wooden table surrounded by plain wooden chairs sat in the centre. She wrestled to her feet the moment she learned of Ginger's presence by the door and bobbed.

"Hello, madam," she said, flushing red with embarrassment. "I was just taking a little break after the luncheon for the mistress."

"Of course. You're entitled to rest. I'm just wondering if there are any leftovers for myself and Miss Higgins?

"Indeed, madam. I can whip you something up in a jiffy. I'll get Phyllis to bring it to you in the morning room."

"That would be fabulous. Thank you."

By the time Ginger and Haley had returned, they found two hot beef and mushroom pies waiting.

"Oh, Bossy," Ginger said to her little pet as he followed her into the cheery morning room. "It smells scrumptious, doesn't it?"

She cut a small portion of the pie, put it onto the saucer of her teacup, and set it on the floor. Boss's stub of a tail shimmied with thanks.

The meat pie was delectable—the morsels of beef tender and juicy. The slices of mushroom added a savoury tang.

Ginger moaned with delight. "Mrs. Beasley is a master."

Haley agreed. "A person could definitely get used to this," she said as she lifted another forkful of pie to her mouth.

"To what? Eating?"

"To being waited on hand and foot," Haley replied. "I've barely had to scrape a meal together since I arrived in England." She lifted her water glass in a mock toast. "Thanks to you, Lady Gold. I'm afraid I'm growing too accustomed. I'll simply starve to death when I get back to Boston and have to feed myself."

"You'd jolly well better eat up now while you can. Store up on reserves, like the bears in New England that prepare for winter."

Haley cut another slice of her pie. "Good idea."

"Were you and Dr. Guthrie able to establish time of death?" Ginger asked.

Haley hummed. "It's hard to say because the body temperature was reduced by the cold water, so decomposition indicators won't be accurate. Since Miss Ashton was last seen alive when the dance ended at midnight, one can assume she died within an hour of that time. It's highly doubtful she left Bray Manor only to return later."

Ginger inclined her head. "And you're certain Miss Ashton didn't die of a bullet wound?"

"Absolutely," Haley said. "A bullet doesn't just disappear. It either escapes through a corresponding exit wound or becomes lodged in the body."

"If she wasn't shot then what happened to her?"

"She was stabbed."

"Stabbed?" Ginger raised a brow. "A crime of passion, then? Not pre-meditated?"

Haley shrugged. "The injury was caused by something circular. Not a regular blade."

"Curious."

Ginger's gaze moved to the lake stirring in the wind beyond the window. "Let's go and see if the murder scene can tell us more."

As if reading her mind, Phyllis knocked. "Can I be of assistance?"

"Yes, please do gather our outer things from the entrance hall. Miss Higgins and I are going for a stroll."

Outside, the waves on Livingston Lake churned as the wind blew over the surface. Ginger held the scarf she'd draped over her head tightly at her neck. She and Haley stood on the patio beside the French windows of the dance hall as Boss sniffed the surrounding area.

"You couldn't see the lake from this position last night," Ginger said. "The clouds obscured the moon."

"Is it safe to assume Miss Ashton entered the garden from this part of the house?"

"The other rooms were locked to the public. The only other way out was through the front door, on the road side."

Haley peered out towards the spot where the body had been discovered. Police tape tied to wooden stakes rattled in the wind. "That's quite the distance to go in the dark."

"The jetty is closer. The killer could've pushed her in, and the waves washed her to shore. The weather was blustery overnight."

"She also could've been killed elsewhere, her body carried to the jetty and tossed in."

Ginger followed Haley across the lawn and onto the slick surface of the weather-worn jetty. Both the lawn and jetty were slippery when wet, and Ginger was glad she'd agreed to wear the less-than-fashionable thick-soled rubber boots that Phyllis had unearthed. Boss scampered to catch up with them, and Ginger worried he would skid right off the edge. Good thing dogs could swim because Ginger didn't fancy the idea of jumping into the cold water to rescue him. Thankfully, Boss had the sense to stop before any drastic measures were necessary.

Despite Ambrosia's insistence otherwise, Livingston Lake really was more of a pond. The water's edge was framed with reeds that poked through the surface, nesting places for a good number of birds. A small boathouse rested about fifty feet away and two rowing boats could be spotted inside from where Ginger stood.

A number of sturdy looking reeds sprouted up around the jetty. "Could a reed have created the puncture wound?" Ginger asked.

"Technically, yes. However, the victim was killed before she landed in the water, and there were no other signs of trauma that could've indicated cause of death."

"What about poisoning? Someone could've slipped her something and taken her outside to die before dropping her in the lake. Maybe she was punctured on the way in."

"That's possible," Haley said. "I'll suggest to Dr. Guthrie that he test the stomach contents."

Ginger squatted low to study the edge of the jetty, looking for some sign of a struggle. A ripped garment or an item that might have fallen off of the killer. She could see nothing unusual, not on the jetty or in the shallow waters alongside it. And not a single damaged reed.

"I don't think she was on the jetty," Ginger said. "I think she was walking along the shore and the killer sneaked up and stabbed her."

They left the jetty and followed the shoreline.

"You said it was too dark to see the lake," Haley said.

"It was when I came out, but the clouds obscured the moon. It was only a quarter-moon, but it would've shed enough light if there were a break in the clouds."

"A crime of opportunity, then?" Haley said. "The killer couldn't have possibly arranged for Angela to be outside alone just as the clouds broke."

"These are modern times," Ginger said. "The killer could simply have used a torch."

"A torch?"

"A flashlight, my American friend."

CHAPTER 12

*B*efore long, it was time for Ginger to shuttle Haley back to the train station.

Haley held on to her hat while shouting above the Humber's engine. "I really wish I could stay, Ginger, but I promised Dr. Watts I'd be back Monday morning to help him with the new cadavers arriving. Plus, lectures have started up again."

"Of course you must go back," Ginger said. "Besides, Scotland Yard is getting involved. There's nothing more you can do here."

Haley poked Ginger in the arm. "Don't worry. I won't bring up *Inspector Reed* again." Ginger just shook her head. Haley believed Basil Reed to be faking his marital status since a wife had never materialised. Perhaps to keep unwanted female attention at bay. Ginger thought the whole idea romantic foolishness, so unbecoming to one such as Haley who prided herself on being a facts and figures type.

"Instead of worrying about my love life, Miss Higgins, why not get one of your own."

Haley snorted. "I'm married to my work, Ginger, you know that. No man can compete."

Out of nowhere, a flash of brown darted in front of the Humber. Ginger slammed on the brakes and swerved sharply, narrowly missing the pup.

"Ginger!"

Ginger ignored Haley's exclamation and drove on calmly. "I need to return to London soon, too," she said as if the near miss had never happened. "I telephoned Madame Roux earlier and she assured me everything is under control at the shop. It'll only be for a couple more days."

"What's keeping you here?" Haley asked. "Since the Yard is taking over the investigation anyway?"

"I'm worried about Felicia. Naturally, she's shattered by the loss of her friend and with having the tragedy happening at Bray Manor, the poor dear shall never be able to enjoy the view of the lake without envisioning the body there."

"Felicia reminds me a lot of you," Haley said.

"Is that so?" Ginger was surprised by this since she and Felicia weren't related by blood.

Haley regarded her friend with kind eyes. "Yes. You both hide your emotional pain behind a vibrant personality."

Ginger started to protest but stopped. Haley was intelligent and insightful. Instead of denying the statement, Ginger sighed. "I suppose you're right."

The old motorcar jerked to a stop at the station. The Chesterton platform was busy and full of passengers waiting for the last Sunday train to London. A loud whistle announced the steam engine as it snaked toward the station with a final blast of smoke. Haley straightened her skirt and picked up her lone suitcase.

Ginger gave Haley a quick embrace. "Safe travels, my friend."

"And you be careful," Haley said before she stepped onto the train. "There's a killer on the loose and he or she could very well be sleeping at Bray Manor."

That thought was deeply disturbing and even the rattling of the Humber's engine barely scratched Ginger's consciousness. Who among the staff could be a killer? Wilson wore a sense of barely concealed entitlement. Langley appeared to always be looking over her shoulder. Ginger could hardly imagine Mrs. Beasley to be the culprit, but often the least likely of the bunch proves to be the villain.

Phyllis, the most industrious of the lot, had the most opportunity, especially as the poltergeist. As parlour maid, she spent most of her time on the ground floor where the disappearances had occurred.

The engine rumble suddenly turned into an outright hacking cough, snapping Ginger to attention.

The cough was followed by a limp and then a faint as the motorcar came to a full stop.

"*Oh, mercy.*"

Ginger stepped out of the motorcar and unlatched the bonnet. At least the rain had turned to a mere mist, and her wool coat wouldn't be ruined.

The war had forced people to learn about things they'd never dreamed of, especially for the women, and fixing the engines of old French vehicles came with the territory. However, everything in British-made cars was reversed, and Ginger had to imagine it like she was looking in the mirror.

She spotted the problem directly. The v-belt to the alternator had snapped off. A careful scan of the roadway confirmed that she was alone. She moved her hand under her slip and quickly detached the silk hose from her garter. It fell to her ankle and she unbuckled the t-strap of her shoe and slipped it off.

Ginger removed her gloves to thread the hose around the alternator and managed to tie a tight knot. The hose would do as a substitute for a short distance, hopefully long enough to get the Humber back to Bray Manor. She could already picture Wilson's barely restrained displeasure when she broke the news.

The distinctive sound of a motorcar engine, much newer than the one she had been fiddling with, grew closer and pulled to a stop at the kerb. Ginger wasn't surprised, as it was natural for a good citizen to offer to help another who was in distress.

She *was* surprised to see Basil Reed step out of a forest-green 1922 Austin 7.

"Lovely motorcar," she said.

Basil wore a knee-length wool coat with wide lapels, and a full belt tied at the waist, a fashion taken from the military, emphasizing his broad shoulders and manly physique.

It'd been several weeks since she'd seen him last. His hazel eyes were bright with amusement, lines fanning out toward his temples, which were sprinkled with silver. Her heart rate jumped on seeing him and her hands grew moist. She cursed herself for allowing the handsome inspector to affect her so.

He tipped his triply.

"Yours is . . . one of the originals?" he asked, sounding coy.

"I expect so." Ginger realised she was playing with the curl that rested against her cheek and quickly dropped her hand to her side. "So they *did* send you."

His eyes twinkled. "Apparently, I was a special request."

"Hmm," Ginger said, her chin jutting into the air. "Not so special."

Basil's lips twitched as he held in a grin. He nodded to the jalopy behind Ginger. "Do you need a lift?"

"Actually, I was just about to get it started."

"Is that so?" He stepped toward the opened engine and looked. Ginger saw the moment Basil realised she must be short one stocking as his gaze quickly moved from the alternator to her bare foot in her shoe that peeked out from under her coat. She pretended not to notice and instead put on her gloves.

With Basil there to turn the crankshaft, Ginger didn't have to hop in and out.

The Humber began to purr and Ginger flashed Basil a wide smile of success.

"I'll follow you," Basil said. "Make sure the old girl doesn't give up on you again."

"Thank you, "Ginger returned. "And I'm sure you're eager to see the scene of the crime."

CHAPTER 13

*G*inger drove up the long circular drive in front of Bray Manor with Basil following close behind. The old Humber acted up a couple of times and Ginger feared another round of humiliation was imminent. But the motorcar trundled along, happily proving her wrong.

The rain started again, and Ginger made quick strides to the protective overhang over the door. Wilson must've been watching for her as he opened the door before she could place her hand on the handle.

"Wilson, here you are!" She held out the keys, and the butler greedily accepted them. "I'm afraid we've had a little incident with the Humber."

Wilson's sombre expression deepened.

"It's just a broken v-belt, easy to fix. I might put it in the garage, and then call a mechanic to come out."

She motioned to Basil. "This is Inspector Reed. I'm sure he'd appreciate having his motorcar protected from the weather."

"Yes, madam."

Wilson waited for Basil to release his keys, but Basil shook his head. "I won't be staying long. I've booked a room at the Chesterton Inn. I could return early in the morning to start with my inquiries."

"You'll do no such thing," Ginger said. "You must stay here. We have plenty of rooms. I'm sure Ambrosia wouldn't mind."

"No, I shouldn't."

"Why not? The crime scene is here. The suspects are quite likely to be connected to the people here. It just makes sense. And Ambrosia would be sure to be comforted with a law keeper about."

Basil relented and handed his keys to the butler. "Very well. I'll accept."

Ginger turned back to Wilson. "Please find Phyllis and ask her to prepare a room for the inspector." Wilson took Basil's overcoat and hat and hung them on the coat rack before leaving.

Ginger showed Basil to the sitting room, happy to see that the fire burned brightly, and the room was comfortably warm. "Let's have a drink, shall we? And I'll tell you everything I know so far." She opened the glass cabinet above the sideboard and removed two glasses.

"Gin and tonic, isn't it?" She'd remembered his

cocktail choice from a previous and equally calamitous affair.

"Yes, thank you."

"How was the drive up to Chesterton?" Ginger asked as she prepared the drink.

"Rather nice. The weather only dampened at the halfway mark. It's not often I get to drive on open roads."

Ginger handed him his cocktail.

"Thank you."

She gave him a nod then took a sip of her merlot. "Shall I begin?"

Basil crossed his legs at the knee and settled in for the retelling. "Please do."

Aware of her one bare leg, Ginger slipped off her shoes and tucked her feet under her as she curled into Ambrosia's chair—surely, the older woman was sufficiently fatigued and tucked away in bed by now.

Boss, having heard his mistress's voice, sauntered into the room and took his favourite spot in front of the fireplace.

"The reason Haley and I came here was because of an urgent message from Miss Gold. Apparently, there is a poltergeist residing at Bray Manor, and Ambrosia's nerves are in danger of collapsing."

Basil's glass paused midair. "A poltergeist?"

"Ambrosia is convinced that the spirit is real, but I have my own suspicions."

"Do tell."

"To raise funds for the maintenance of Bray Manor, Felicia has organized associations and events to rent rooms—to Ambrosia's mortification. I applaud her entrepreneurial spirit, and Ambrosia isn't so humiliated that she'd stop the flow of money. There are currently three associations that meet weekly: a knitting circle, a gardening group, and a stamp collecting club."

"And you suspect the poltergeist to be one of the association members."

"I initially believed Ambrosia was in need of attention—she can be quite demanding in that respect—and that this new crisis was a ploy to get me to come to Bray Manor."

"Were you hesitant to come?"

Ginger glanced away. She wasn't ready to confess the real reason she'd been reluctant to come. "I've been busy with my new shop."

"But now . . .?"

"I witnessed the trickery first-hand. Someone is having fun at poor Ambrosia's expense. I hadn't had the chance to properly investigate before this tragedy happened."

Basil leaned forward. "What exactly happened at the ball?"

"Dancing mostly. You would've enjoyed it." Ginger smiled at the memory of the dances she and Basil had shared on the SS *Rosa* where they'd first met when she came to England from Boston. "A pleasant mix of social classes, which goes to show you how great the changes are that the Great War has brought us. Before 1914, a mixed event like that would never have happened."

Basil removed a notebook from his suit pocket and referred to something he'd written inside. "Were you acquainted with the victim, Miss Ashton?"

"I met her for the first time at the dance. She was a friend of Felicia's. She and another girl with them, a Miss Muriel Webb."

"What are your impressions of Miss Webb?"

"I would say that Miss Webb lacked the confidence of which Miss Ashton, and of course Felicia, were in possession. I got the feeling that she tried a little too hard to fit in. Miss Ashton was what one would call a serious flapper."

Basil stared back with a look of confusion. "Meaning?"

"She just wanted to have fun and nothing else."

"Right. Did you notice anything out of the ordinary? Unusual behaviour? Strange conversations?"

"Well, now that you mention it, Miss Ashton was quite hostile towards Miss Webb. Her back was turned to me at the time, so she didn't know I'd witnessed the confrontation."

"What was the nature of the conflict?"

"Miss Ashton accused Miss Webb of not being able to think for herself. She used unkind language to express it."

Basil shifted in his chair, crossing the other leg. "What else do you know about our victim?"

"She was engaged to Mr. Croft and would have become a Baroness once Lord Croft dies."

Basil's eyebrows jumped at the news. "I dare say."

Ginger sipped her wine. She nibbled her lip in contemplation. Something else bothered her. Or rather *someone*. She wished she could avoid discussing him with Basil. She watched the fire, delaying the inevitable.

Basil was a good investigator, and it didn't take long before he probed. "Is there something more, Ginger?"

Ginger sighed and turned back to face him. "Felicia's been walking out with a Captain Smithwick."

Basil frowned. "Francis Smithwick?"

"Do you know him?"

"He and I served in the same regiment." Just as he lifted his drink to his lips he added, "For a short time."

"He was there last night, and I saw him having a terse conversation with Miss Ashton. At one point he grabbed her by the wrist."

"So not strangers to each other."

"No," Ginger said tightly.

"And you're worried the captain might be involved with other women, possibly with Miss Ashton." The inspector's intuition was spot-on, Ginger thought. He added with particular sensitivity, "You're worried that Felicia might get her heart broken."

"Not might, Basil. *Will*. She definitely will."

Basil regarded her carefully. "Are you personally acquainted with Captain Smithwick?"

"No," she said without thought, then sighed again. Solving this case might depend on her complete honesty. "Yes. We met in France."

"Were you *involved*?"

"No! Of course not. I was married."

"I didn't mean to offend. I just thought that would explain your worry for Felicia."

"Right. I do apologise. It was a reasonable question."

"I assume Mr. Croft was at the dance as well?"

"Yes. He and I were dancing when the altercation occurred. He intercepted.

"A complicated affair."

"Indeed. His mother, the Honourable Mrs. Croft was also present. Mr. Croft, her husband, passed away before the war."

"I imagine the Honourable Mrs. Croft isn't too keen on the engagement?"

"I suspect not. I witnessed more than one dirty look exchanged between them."

The war had made the world smaller. How coincidental that both she and Basil had met Captain Smithwick in France, and now, the three of them together in Chesterton mixed up with a murder.

Ginger couldn't help but wonder just how coincidental it actually was. Smithwick was a strategist. She could safely assume he had investigated her since her return to London and had discovered her connection to the inspector. Could she, Basil, *and* Felicia all be pawns in an elaborate setup?

Ginger collected Basil's empty glass and set it beside her own on the sideboard.

"I should like to start interviews first thing in the morning, starting with Miss Ashton's family," Basil said as he stood.

"Do you mind if I join you?"

Basil grinned with a look of surrender. "I'd be shocked if it were otherwise."

CHAPTER 14

The scribbled map, drawn by a sleepy Felicia, led Ginger and Basil to a middle-class area of family houses snuggled together in small plots. Basil pulled up to a tired-looking red brick building, in need of some tender loving care.

Ginger was astounded. "This is Miss Ashton's home?" She studied the map again, wondering if they'd somehow made a wrong turn, but the directions were simple.

"You're surprised a member of the peerage would marry a girl from the middle-class?"

"Well, yes. I know it sounds snobbish, but pre-war, this would've been an outright scandal in these parts. It's still considered scandalous by many. No wonder Mrs. Croft was so against the union. The question is why did Patrick Croft get involved with Angela Ashton in the first place?"

Not for the same reason Sir Daniel Gold had got involved with her—money. Ginger's father, George Hartigan, had been a successful businessman and a shrewd investor. He had known Daniel's parents before they died and had kept in touch with the family. Daniel came to Boston to meet Ginger on George Hartigan's invitation. Perhaps her father had known by then that he was ill and wanted to make sure Ginger was taken care of after he died. His views were stuck in the Victorian times, where women needed men to provide and care for them whilst they busied themselves with raising children and running charitable events. George provided the money, Daniel provided security.

"The war made lovers of the rebellious who were prone to do impulsive and drastic things," Basil said. "Especially with the youth."

"That's true," Ginger said. No one thought she and Daniel would actually fall in love.

Basil waved a hand in question. "After all this time, why not just break it off?"

"It's a matter of honour, I suppose," Ginger said. "At least for Mr. Croft. For Miss Ashton, it was most certainly a matter of money and prestige."

Basil agreed. "Certainly a step up from this." Basil knocked on the front door, which was opened by a red-eyed woman in her mid-thirties.

"I'm Chief Inspector Reed from Scotland Yard,

and this is Lady Gold. I'm sorry to intrude on your grief, but if I may have a moment?"

The woman's lips twitched nervously as she welcomed them in. "I'm Mrs. Cecil Dunsbury, Angela's older sister. As you can imagine, we're all completely distraught to have lost her so suddenly and in such a horrid manner."

"My deepest condolences on behalf of all the members of the household at Bray Manor," Ginger said. "We deeply regret that an event held there has been the source of your sorrow."

"It's hardly your fault, but thank you."

Mrs. Dunsbury brought them tea. "My mother is resting. You can imagine she didn't sleep well last night. Neither of us did."

"Do you live nearby?" Ginger asked. "It's so good that you could come to be with your mother at a time like this."

"Yes, on the other side of Chesterton. I left the young 'uns with the neighbours. My husband took over the butcher's shop when my father passed away."

A large grandfather clock struck the hour and they waited for the eleven chimes to ring. The intrusion created an awkward pause. Ginger blew on her tea and sipped.

When the last chime rang, Basil cleared his throat. "Mrs. Dunsbury, did your sister have any enemies?"

Ginger was surprised when Mrs. Dunsbury didn't quickly object. Instead, after a pause, she said, "My sister had a dramatic personality. She attracted and repelled quite equally."

"I understand she was to be married soon?" Basil said.

The twitching about Mrs. Dunsbury's mouth worsened. "In the spring. The third postponement I'm afraid. My mother was beside herself."

"Why's that?" Ginger had to force herself not to stare at Mrs. Dunsbury's mouth. It seemed to work non-stop. Did the woman not notice?

Mrs. Dunsbury's eyes scanned the modest room. "Not to be brash, but Angela's marriage into the Croft family would have changed everything for us. And it's not like there are a lot of eligible men around." Her lips seemed to work against her, and Ginger marvelled that the woman got any words out at all.

"Despite Angela's beauty, she wasn't likely to get a better offer. Mother just couldn't understand Angela's reluctance, and quite frankly, neither could I."

"What was Angela's reason for the postponement?" Basil asked.

"She found Mr. Croft . . . unattractive." Mrs. Dunsbury's eyes flashed with shame. "The poor man was wounded in the war! I kept telling her that a man is more than his face and that Mr. Croft was still attractive even with the mask.

"But Angela said he repulsed her, and she wasn't going to marry him until the Baron died and she would immediately become a Baroness. Until then, she just wanted to party and have fun. I'm afraid the girl was spoilt. My father always told her how pretty she was, and in truth, she never was held accountable for her frequent outlandish behaviour. If Father were alive, he might've been able to talk some sense into her."

Mrs. Dunsbury sobbed softly, touching her face with a linen handkerchief, hiding her quivering lips. "And now she's dead. I just can't believe someone would . . . assault her in this way. It's just so inconceivable!"

Ginger couldn't imagine losing her younger half-sister, Louisa, who remained in Boston with Ginger's step-mother, or Felicia, her younger sister through marriage. She commiserated. "It's such a senseless tragedy."

Basil wasn't affected by the woman's tears. "An inquest has been scheduled for Wednesday afternoon, Mrs. Dunsbury, and your evidence shall be required. Please stay in Chesterton until then."

CHAPTER 15

*O*nce back in the Austin, Basil turned to Ginger and asked, "What are your thoughts on that?"

Ginger pulled on the cuffs of her leather gloves, tightening the fit. "Apparently, Miss Ashton wasn't well-liked by all. Her sister obviously cared for her, but even she couldn't keep her feelings of disappointment entirely hidden."

"Was Mrs. Dunsbury at the dance?"

"I didn't notice her, but that doesn't mean she wasn't there."

The older sister didn't have the beauty or charisma of the younger. Angela could fill the room with her presence, where, Ginger feared, Mrs. Dunsbury was more like the librarian, Miss Smith. Easy to overlook. "The hall was full," she added as an excuse.

"Righto," Basil said. He started up the Austin, and it chugged to life. "Next stop, Heather's End."

Heather's End was the impressive Croft family home. Unlike Bray Manor, it wasn't as old as the heather-covered fields, which sprawled out behind it. The exterior was modern and white with clean straight lines and shiny black wrought iron railings around the balconies on the second floor. The landscaping was neat and tidy, and a marble water fountain, turned off for the winter, filled the centre of the circular drive. It was immediately obvious that Heather's End had more money invested into the upkeep than Bray Manor had.

The heavy wooden door opened to a long-faced butler. "The family isn't taking visitors."

Basil displayed his badge. "I'm Chief Inspector Reed from Scotland Yard. I'm investigating a murder. Please allow me to enter."

The butler stood aside, and though he was shorter than Basil, he somehow managed to look down his nose. "Please wait here."

The entrance hall was massive, twice the size of Bray Manor with the sound attributes of a cave. Ginger and Basil did not talk for fear of being overheard.

The butler returned and guided them to the drawing room. "Your name, madam?" he asked.

"Lady Gold."

The butler swung the door to the drawing room open and announced, "Chief Inspector Reed and Lady Gold," then bowed and stepped back into the passage.

Though Mrs. Croft stared at them with surprise, Patrick Croft crossed the room with a relaxed gait, as if he had expected them, and shook both of their hands. "Chief Inspector Reed. Lady Gold, it's a pleasure."

"I'm sorry for the circumstances," Ginger said.

"As am I. Believe me."

Ginger approached Mrs. Croft who sat stiffly in her chair as if in shock. "This must be so dreadful for you all," she said as she claimed an empty armchair beside the older woman.

"I'm just so . . . stunned, Lady Gold. Who could do such a ghastly thing?"

"This is what we're attempting to find out," Ginger said kindly. "The inspector would like to ask a few questions."

"Yes, of course," Mrs. Croft said as if sense was beginning to register.

Looking stylish in an argyle sweater and sporty tweed plus fours—later Ginger would describe the trousers to Haley as knickerbockers four inches below the knee—Patrick Croft stood casually by the fireplace, lighting a pipe. After the bowl was aglow, he let out a puff of smoke and said, "I suppose you want to ask me for an alibi. I was at the dance, Lady Gold can attest to that. I came home with Mother after the dance. Our butler drove us."

"When was the last time you saw Miss Ashton alive?" Basil asked.

"About midnight, I'd say. She'd finally saved a dance for me. I do think she intended to dance with every available man in the room."

"Why didn't you take her home?" Ginger asked.

"I wanted to. But Angela said she was spending the night as Miss Gold's guest."

"If you don't mind my saying so," Basil said, "you don't seem too aggrieved by Miss Ashton's death."

"Of course I'm aggrieved, but only because an innocent girl was cut down so violently in her prime. I'd be lying if I said I was in love with her."

"Why did you not break off the engagement?" Basil asked.

"I tried to. I thought that she'd want to get out of it . . . after this," Mr. Croft said pointing to the injured side of his face. But she'd have none of it."

"She was a gold-digger," Mrs. Croft said scathingly.

"Mother!"

"I don't mean to speak ill of the dead, but that's the truth!"

"At any rate," Mr. Croft said. "Angela insisted that I go through with the wedding, and I didn't fight her on it. I'm not bound to get any other takers, and at least there would've been a possibility of my producing an heir."

"You didn't mind her seeing other men?" Basil asked.

Mr. Croft inhaled deeply of his pipe and let out a long billow of smoke. "What man wouldn't mind that, Inspector? But if you're suggesting I killed her, you're wrong." He settled into a nearby chair and casually crossed his legs, displaying his knee-high knitted socks and brown carpet slippers. "If I were you," he said after another puff on his pipe, "I'd talk to Francis Smithwick."

Ginger tensed at the mention of the captain's name. "Why?"

"He and Angela were . . . friends. But I suspect their *friendship* had grown sour recently."

"Oh?" Basil said.

"They had . . . words, at the dance." He nodded to Ginger. "Lady Gold was a witness."

"I understand you rescued her from that indelicate situation," Basil stated.

"Yes, but Angela was a stubborn girl and wouldn't tell me what they were talking about."

Patrick Croft extinguished his pipe in the ashtray on the end table and stood.

"I'm sorry, Inspector, that's all I know. Now if you don't mind, both Mother and I are rather exhausted."

Basil and Ginger drove by a tea shop, and Basil suggested luncheon. Ginger delighted in the cosy room with low ceilings and exposed brick walls. It was connected to a bookshop where patrons could purchase reading material to read along with their tea, should they be inclined. A couple of centuries old, the room was quaint, and smelled deliciously of homemade soup and flaky buns.

"Boston has charming old restaurants," she said, taking the room in. "But nothing quite as authentic as this. And no public houses, of course, with prohibition. At least, none that advertise as such."

"Do you miss Boston very much?" Basil asked.

"Not as much as I thought I would. I'm surprised at how fast I'm settling into London life."

"I hear you've opened a dress shop."

Ginger smiled with the pride of a new mother. "I have and it's fabulous. I do need to get back soon. It's in its infant stages and I should be there."

Basil lowered his chin and stated, "I'm afraid you're stuck here until the inquest."

Ginger sighed. "I know. Feathers & Flair is in good hands with my shop manager, Madame Roux."

Their order arrived. Ginger peeled off her gloves and stored them in her handbag.

The chicken soup was delicious, and they drank it eagerly. Ginger had to refrain from emitting a juvenile "mmm."

"Getting back to the case," Basil said as he

wiped his jaw with a serviette. "Mr. Croft had motive and opportunity. He felt socially trapped into a marriage to a woman who threw herself at other men in his presence. She wouldn't let him go, so he killed her."

"But what were his means?" Ginger asked. In her heart, she just couldn't picture Mr. Croft as a killer. Though she'd learned that many things were not what they seemed, and Mr. Croft had been a soldier and therefore *had* killed before.

"It would help if we could find a murder weapon," Basil said. "Miss Ashton was stabbed, but not with a blade. If this were France, I'd say she was impaled with a bayonet."

Ginger dropped her spoon.

"Ginger?"

"Captain Smithwick. He has an army rifle with a bayonet."

"How do you know?"

"He's bragged about it to me in the past. He's quite proud of his war collection."

Basil frowned. "All army weapons were to be returned at the end of the war."

"True. But, not all were."

A new shop assistant arrived and busied herself in the bookshop. Ginger could see into the shop from her position in the tea room and stared.

"Is something wrong?"

"That's Felicia's friend, Muriel Webb, from the

dance. She looks so different dressed reservedly I almost didn't recognise her."

Basil twisted his neck to look. "Your sister keeps interesting company."

"These girls met during the war," Ginger explained. "Everyone wanted to serve in some capacity, and the girls from Chesterton weren't exempt. Status had no part to play. All anyone cared about was the war and doing their bit. There were four of them at the same farm, though Felicia was younger than the others. They delivered messages. They delivered vegetables from the garden to people who hadn't means to food. It was hard and demanding work from dawn to dusk. Everyone had greasy hair and dirty fingernails. The experience bound the girls together in a way not even class could separate."

Ginger sipped her tea, her mind niggling at something. "Felicia mentioned that one of the girls died. I immediately assumed it was due to sickness, the Spanish Flu hit this region quite hard during that time." She leaned forward and lowered her voice. "I remember now that the girl committed suicide. The family wanted it hushed up, and that's why it slipped my mind."

"Sadly, the end of the war didn't bring joy to those who'd lost loved ones," Basil said. "Indeed, many have found it hard to go on with life since."

"I imagine you've seen your fair share of suicide cases," Ginger said.

Basil's sadness mirrored Ginger's. "More than my fair share, I'd say."

Muriel Webb entered the tea room and ordered some tea for herself. Ginger called out to her, "Miss Webb!" She waved a hand, adding, "Hello!"

Muriel approached cautiously. "Hello, Lady Gold. How splendid to see you again."

"My friend and I were out and decided to stop for a bite to eat. This is Chief Inspector Reed from Scotland Yard."

Muriel blanched at the introduction. "I'm afraid I must get back to the bookshop—"

"Miss Webb," Basil said. "If I could just have a moment of your time. I'll speak to your management if it's a problem."

Muriel hesitated, then stepped closer. "Sir?"

"I understand you were close to the girl who died last night at Bray Manor."

Muriel's eyes shuttered closed. "I can't believe it's true." She stared back at him. "Who would do such a thing?"

"It's been said that Miss Ashton wasn't always pleasant to be around."

"What? That's a lie. Angela was the most wonderful of people, like a sister to me." She scowled deeply. "That war has brought the evil out of everyone."

"Can you think of anyone who might want to hurt Miss Ashton?"

"No. Well . . . no."

"Are you sure?"

"Yes, now I really do have to get back to work. Please excuse me."

Miss Webb scurried away forgetting her own order.

"Did you find her behaviour rather odd?" Ginger asked.

"Indeed. She's frightened of something. Or someone."

"Can't be Angela Ashton any longer."

Basil took a sip of his tea. "Devil or angel, our Miss Ashton. It depends on who you talk to."

The table behind them was obscured by a large planter, so Ginger hadn't noticed the occupant before. A man in uniform slid out and approached them. "I hate to interrupt, but I couldn't help but overhear." Ginger couldn't hold in her shock at the sight of Captain Smithwick towering over them. He leaned in and whispered, "Muriel Webb is a liar. She hated Angela Ashton's guts."

CHAPTER 16

*G*inger and Basil stared hard at the captain.

"How long have you been listening in?" Basil asked tersely.

"Long enough," Smithwick said, taking a chair beside Ginger. His closeness made the hairs on her neck stand on end, and she quickly shifted over.

"I didn't see you there," Ginger said. She had looked, too. Something about being reacquainted with Smithwick had her secret ops training coming to the fore. She had automatically scanned the room on entering. The table behind them had definitely been vacant.

Smithwick chuckled as he pulled out a rolled cigarette and lit it with a brass lighter. "You're losing your edge, Ginger. I happened to have been in the gents when you came in. I recognised you—your fancy hat caught my eye—but you had your nose in the menu." He stretched out his legs and let out a stream of smoke. "Quite honestly, I thought I'd overhear the two of you making love, but it seems you were telling me the truth yesterday when you said there wasn't anyone else."

Ginger's eyes burned with embarrassment and she wanted to kick the captain for his arrogance and his familiarity—calling her by her Christian name as if he were close to her.

"Now that your stupid curiosity has been satisfied," she spat, "you can leave."

"Actually, Lady Gold," Basil said. "I'd like to ask the captain a few questions."

Smithwick chuckled, tapped ash into the ashtray, and held the cigarette in the air between two nicotine-stained fingers. "Fire away."

"What makes you say that Miss Webb is a liar?"

"I've had the opportunity to spend time with her friend, Miss Gold." He grinned coyly at Ginger and she swallowed back the fury she felt.

"Miss Webb is the ugly sister of the three."

"Dear Lord, Captain Smithwick!" Ginger said.

"I don't mean to be a cad, but it's true. Muriel Webb has barely concealed her jealousy. Angela was the prettiest, and Felicia the wealthiest. Miss Webb despised them both." Smithwick inhaled and released a puff of smoke from the corner of his mouth. "Really, *Lady Gold*, I thought you more discerning."

"Captain Smithwick," Basil said, drawing the

man's attention back to himself. "Are you in possession of a rifle fitted with a bayonet?"

Smithwick chortled. "As you well know, all firearms and weapons used on the battlefield belong to the British Army."

"Answer the question, please."

"Why, yes, I am, and I did hear Lady Gold give away my confidences." He clucked at her and shook his head." Nursing his cigarette, he continued, "King and country are under the impression the rifle was lost in France. I had to pay for it of course." He snickered. "Believe me, I wasn't the only one to have 'lost' something in France. What does this have to do with anything?"

"Miss Ashton was stabbed to death."

"Ah, I see. Have you enquired of Mr. Croft?" The captain butted his cigarette out in the tray. "He also has a goodly collection of 'lost' war items? Don't be fooled by that mask of his. He's an opportunist, even without a face."

Ginger snorted. "He was going to marry a woman who would bring nothing to the marriage. How is that opportunistic?"

Smithwick laughed as he stood to leave. "He doesn't have to marry her now, does he?"

Basil called after him. "You won't mind if I view your 'lost' war items, Captain Smithwick?"

Smithwick tipped his hat. "Knock yourself out, old chap."

Ginger held a glass of water against her flaming cheeks.

Basil regarded her curiously. "That man has really got under your skin."

"I can't stand that he's involved with Felicia. It literally makes me sick."

"Do you think he killed Miss Ashton?"

"He's certainly a suspect. After all, the man has killed before."

"I do hope you mean on the battlefield."

Not exactly, but Ginger didn't want to get into that. "He can't be trusted."

Basil leaned back and considered her. "You two obviously have history. Can you tell me what happened?"

Ginger sighed. "Maybe someday, Inspector."

Basil paid the bill as they left. He opened the passenger door of the Austin for Ginger and she climbed in.

"What do you want to do now?" she asked

His eyes flashed with compassion. "I think it's time we spoke to Miss Gold."

Dear, dear Felicia. Ginger had hoped to keep her out of things but relented. "I know you're right. Just be gentle with her. She's been through a lot."

Ginger unpinned her hat and tossed it onto the bench in the entrance hall of Bray Manor. Wilson, hearing Ginger and Basil enter, offered his assistance.

"Where might I find Miss Gold?" Ginger asked.

The butler answered without emotion. "Miss Gold left about ten minutes ago."

"Did she say where she was going?"

"No, madam. Only that she'd be out for the rest of the day."

Ginger had noticed the garage doors were closed and assumed the Humber was tucked away safely inside. Besides, it had yet to see a mechanic.

"With whom did she go?" Ginger had a sinking feeling she knew the answer.

"A Captain Smithwick called for her, madam."

"Thank you, Wilson," Ginger said in dismissal.

Ginger led Basil to the sitting room where they took either end of the settee. "What a beast!" Ginger said. "The moment he left us he hurried over here to whisk Felicia away. I don't know what kind of game he's playing, but I could throttle the man."

"Perhaps Felicia knows something he doesn't want her to tell us?"

"Undoubtedly."

"Do you want to go after them?"

Boss hopped onto Ginger's lap, and she stroked his little black head. "Felicia would disown me if we did that."

"But, do you think she's in danger? I could call the locals to look out for them."

"I don't think she's in danger," Ginger said. Though if Smithwick killed Angela Ashton, then she very well could be. "But, yes, call the police as a caution."

Boss at her heels, Ginger showed Basil the telephone room—a study-like space with a leather couch and matching chair. On a circular end table stood a candlestick phone. Ginger was pretty sure that Felicia was the only member of the house to actually take advantage of the modern convenience. She was glad Daniel had insisted on it being installed.

Restless, Ginger meandered to the window. Ambrosia was in the flower gardens overseeing Clement. He busied himself with a pair of secateurs, what Haley would call garden clippers, preparing the beds for winter. The weather was moody and evocative. Low-lying clouds and a rolling mist floated along the lake, but no rain. She remembered the rowing boats in the boathouse.

When Basil ended his call, she turned to him. "Would you like to go out on the lake?"

CHAPTER 17

*L*ike the skin of a drum on a winter's day, Ginger's chest tightened. She felt trapped in Bray Manor, senselessly claustrophobic. The waves called to her, lapping through the grass, slapping against the jetty. Perhaps, out there, she could breathe.

Basil stared at her, his hazel eyes registering surprise at her suggestion to venture out. "Isn't it raining?"

"Just a drizzle," Ginger said. "Besides, it's calming. It might clear our heads so we can get to the bottom of this awful business."

"Let's go, then." Basil disappeared into the entrance hall to gather their coats and scarves and returned waving two umbrellas. "I pulled these from the brolly rack, just in case."

Ginger gathered the wool blanket that hung over

the back of the settee, and called to Boss. "Hey, lazy-bones," she said. "We're going outside!" The pup scampered to his feet and followed Ginger and Basil out of the French windows into the garden. A pair of rubber boots had been left on the patio, and Ginger took a moment to slip them on. Much more suitable than the strappy shoes she'd been wearing.

Together Ginger and Basil pulled the rowing boat out of the boathouse. Basil guided it by the rope towards the jetty as Ginger collected the oars.

The fog swirled above their heads. With a deep breath, Ginger inhaled the fresh air—a mix of old earth, damp trees and lake mildew. The tension in her chest gave way little by little. "I know everyone gets so excited when the sun shines," she said, "but I'm rather fond of the moody atmosphere. It's brooding and mysterious."

"It's mysterious all right," Basil said as he helped her into the small boat. "One can barely see beyond one's nose."

Boss jumped in and onto Ginger's lap. Basil sat at the back of the boat and pushed off the jetty with one oar. They slipped quietly through the water. Ginger found the sounds of nature soothing to the disquieted churning within. Geese skimmed along the lake surface squawking out their disapproval at this inter-ruption. Boss let out a string of short barks, encour-aging the fowl onward. Smaller birds sang, their high-pitched trilling echoing along the lake's surface.

"The reed bunting nests here." Ginger pointed to a cluster of reeds poking out of the water, and the small grey bird singing with a loud, beautiful voice.

Basil watched the bunting in its habitat with appreciation. "Lake Livingston *is* more of a large pond, isn't it?"

Ginger grinned. "Don't let Ambrosia hear you say that."

Basil paddled with slow, intense strokes, and Ginger relaxed into the sound of the wooden blades lapping through the water. The vice-like anxiety squeezing her ribs was nearly gone.

Ginger knew it wasn't the case that was troubling her, though she did have grave concerns about Felicia's life choices. It was the little graveyard on the other side of the lake, the marble crosses visible from their position.

Basil followed her gaze and stated plainly, "You miss him."

"I do," Ginger admitted. "It's been five years since the war took him, but at times it feels like yesterday."

"It must be hard for you to be here, at his family home."

Ginger was tempted to make light of the matter, but the look on Basil's face was . . . vulnerable. Instead, she answered honestly. "Yes. In Boston, I could pretend that Daniel was simply 'away.' I talked to him, to his photograph, as if we were on the telephone." Ginger didn't know why she was being so candid about her private life, but it felt good to confess. "I rather liked my delusion. Coming to London and especially here, to Bray Manor . . . is hard."

Basil said nothing, only paddled, long strokes of the blades cutting smoothly through the water's surface. His hands were red from the cold. His gold wedding ring stood out in sharp contrast.

A window of transparency had opened between them, almost as the fog seemed to close in and Ginger stepped through it, daring to tread on very personal ground. "What about you? Do you miss your wife?"

Basil's hazel eyes flashed with remorse. "Yes. Every day."

He paused in his paddling and the boat bobbed with the waves. They sat there in silence and Ginger wasn't sure what she should say to that or *if* she should say anything at all. Basil eventually spoke. "I've decided to give Emilia what she wants. I'm going to divorce her."

Ginger allowed herself to wonder, just for the slightest moment, if Basil's decision had anything to do with his having met her.

"I'm sorry," she said.

Divorce was only granted on grounds of adultery. Often it was the husband who claimed ownership of the indiscretion to preserve the wife's reputation, even if she was in fact the guilty party. Ginger didn't doubt for a moment that Basil would take the blame for the collapse of his marriage.

Basil pulled back on the oars again. "I am, too."

The mist settled in around them, like a cocoon, thick and close, fortifying the sense of intimacy from which they couldn't easily escape. Nor, Ginger realised with some consternation, did she want to. The surrealism caused them both to speak aloud on things they'd never dream of in normal circumstances.

Basil rested the paddles and let the gentle wind carry the boat along where it may. He rubbed his chin where a shadow of late-day bristles formed, then cleared his throat.

"What I don't understand," he said, "is how Angela Ashton died without anyone seeing her, or missing her."

Back to the case. To impersonal matters. Ginger felt as if she and Basil Reed were in a constant dance —moving closer, then farther apart—all at the whim of some invisible band. Hands on shoulder and hip. Hands off.

"The doors to the veranda were opened," she said. "But the weather was cool, so not many people ventured out. The few of us who did go outside didn't stay long."

Basil paddled, *one, two, three* strokes, then rested. "So it's late, people are leaving and, I assume, the band was packing up. The staff are collecting dirty glasses and teacups and delivering them to the kitchen. Miss Gold assumed Miss Ashton had left with Miss Webb. Miss Webb supposed Miss Ashton left with Mr. Croft, and Mr. Croft believed his fiancée was spending the night at Bray Manor."

"The question is," Ginger said, "why did Miss Ashton lie about staying the night. Felicia hadn't extended that invitation to anyone, though now I wonder why not."

"Perhaps Felicia had plans with Captain Smith-wick for after the dance?"

That thought made Ginger's blood chill. "If she did, he stood her up."

"Ah. Perhaps he'd scheduled himself twice. Promised both Miss Gold and Miss Ashton that he'd meet up with them."

"That could be why the captain and Miss Ashton argued," Ginger said.

"Smithwick, having lost control of Miss Ashton, searches for her later, and finds her alone outside and kills her."

Ginger's heart tripped. "*Oh mercy!* Now I'm rather worried for Felicia." Had she let her sister-in-law spend the day with a murderer? Her mind went to the worst places: Smithwick's bayonet, the grizzly stab wound on Angela Ashton's body.

"I think we should go in," she said, a small tremor in her voice giving away her rising panic.

The boat had drifted into the reeds and Basil

worked to paddle them out. Boss barked, his paws up against the edge of the boat.

"What is it, Bossy?" Ginger spotted an empty bird's nest in the reeds, Boss having frightened the occupant off. Then her eyes caught sight of something shimmering on the surface of the water, like an entangled floating pearl.

Reaching over the side of the boat, she plucked out a long smooth wooden stick.

She gasped. "It's Felicia's missing knitting needle!" She held the object outstretched. "See the nail polish on the end?"

"Let me have a look at that." Basil wrapped a handkerchief over his palm for Ginger to place the item on. The tip had been chiselled into a sharp point. Basil frowned. "I think you just found our murder weapon."

CHAPTER 18

*H*aving just been convinced that Felicia was walking out with a murderer, and now being slapped with this new evidence, Ginger reeled from the incongruity. If Angela Ashton was stabbed with a knitting needle, how did Smithwick get his hands on it? And if the murder was premeditated, why on earth use a knitting needle?

It didn't make sense.

Unless the poltergeist was the killer?

Basil paddled swiftly towards the jetty. "Our focus was all wrong," he said.

"We were looking at Miss Ashton's friends," Ginger said, "when we should be looking at the knitting association members."

"Exactly."

"Unless the killer and the poltergeist are

acquainted. It could've been chance that the last 'trick' also provided a good weapon."

Basil assisted Ginger out of the boat, and the moment her boots hit the jetty, her urgency to find Felicia kicked in and she hurried to the house. Boss chased after her with equal intensity. She called over her shoulder to Basil. "Just tie the boat to the piling. I'll get someone to return it to the boathouse later."

Phyllis was dusting the sitting room when Ginger blew in. "Phyllis, have you seen Miss Gold? Has she returned?"

Phyllis shook her head. "I wouldn't know, madam."

Ginger released a grunt of frustration. Basil soon caught up and was at her side. "We could drive around Chesterton. Maybe we'll spot them."

"It's getting dark. By the time we get to town, it will be black out." Chesterton still depended on gas light and they were sparse.

"Is there someone to call?" Basil asked. "Do you know where Smithwick lives?"

"He resides in St. Albans. He must be staying at the Chesterton Inn. It's the only inn in town."

Ginger caught sight of herself in the entrance hall mirror and stopped abruptly. If it weren't for the urgency of the situation, she wouldn't be caught dead going out in public looking as windblown and pale-faced as she did. She sorely wished she could at least tidy up a bit for Inspector Reed's sake. The poor man forced to look at her when she was not at all well put together.

"Is something the matter, madam?"

"Oh, Wilson." Ginger hoped the butler could help. "Have you seen Miss Gold? Has she returned?"

"I'm afraid not."

Basil reached for the door and just as he was about to grasp the handle, the door jerked open, as if the wind had caught it and Felicia breezed inside.

Ginger and Basil stared at the wayward girl, and she stared back, her expression reflecting confusion.

"What's going on?" Her gaze lingered on Ginger. "Are you feeling all right, Ginger. You look flustered."

"I'm fine. We're fine. Frankly, we were about to come and look for you."

"What on earth for? I'm a big girl. Quite able to take care of myself."

Ginger patted at her flyaway hair. "Of course, you are."

Felicia rolled her eyes and lumbered up the staircase. Ginger watched her go, relief drenching her like a sudden downpour. The fear that had gripped her sifted away, along with the strength in her bones.

What she needed now was a stiff drink. She forced a smile. "Inspector, care to join me for some early evening refreshment?"

"I'd be delighted."

"Wilson, perhaps you could see to some food?"

"Certainly, madam."

"Basil, do excuse me for a moment. I'd like to get changed."

Phyllis had unpacked for Ginger when she'd arrived. Was it only three days ago? It felt much longer. She removed her damp clothes and put on an orange silk printed blouse with long, flowy sleeves, a white pleated skirt, and donned clean stockings—snapping them expertly to her garter. She brushed her hair, trained the tips to curl at her cheeks with her fingers, and finished with a fresh coat of mascara and lipstick. Not too much. She didn't want to look like she was trying too hard.

Oh mercy, where did that thought come from?

She wasn't *trying* at all.

Her gaze shot to her night table, and she blinked in bewilderment when the photo of Daniel wasn't there. She'd *forgotten* it.

She'd never forgotten his photo when she travelled before, ever.

Her fingers went to the long strands of beads hanging from her neck and she twisted them around a finger. She felt frozen in place, her emotions a knot of confusion. She was in Daniel's home and *Basil* was downstairs waiting for her.

No. Not waiting for *her*.

Just waiting. A drink before retiring. Another day of investigation ahead of them tomorrow.

That was all.

Ginger shook her head as if dust had truly gathered between her ears, and headed downstairs. She entered the sitting room, casual and composed, as a hostess should.

Basil held the open decanter of brandy and poured two glasses. His eyes lingered on Ginger for a beat before he remembered the extra glass in his hand and offered it to her.

"Thank you." Ginger sat elegantly on a chair. "Such a day!" she added before taking a sip of her brandy.

"Indeed." Basil picked up the poker and stoked the fire. "Where does the knitting association meet?" he asked, getting right down to business.

"They meet here, in the sitting room."

Basil looked at her with surprise. "Do all the associations meet in here?"

"No. Just the knitting circle. Ambrosia is a member, and she prefers to meet in her own home. She likes comfort, and of course, to have final say on things."

Basil crossed to a chair opposite Ginger. "Can you refresh my memory as to who the knitting circle members are?"

"Ambrosia of course, a Mrs. Richards, a Miss Smith, a Miss Whitton, and the Honourable Mrs. Croft."

"Not Miss Gold?"

"She joined the group just for that night, to accompany Haley and me. We attended with the view of nosing out the poltergeist culprit. Felicia was there to spend time with us."

"When did the association last meet?"

"Friday. Just three evenings ago. Goodness, it feels like ages."

"Who noticed the missing knitting needle?"

"I did. Felicia had left her knitting basket behind. Haley was with me."

"Can you give me a run through of what happened that night?"

Ginger smirked. "We knitted."

Basil's mouth pulled up crookedly, then he pressed on. "Did you talk about anything?"

"Ambrosia made introductions, then a bit of gossip. Then the topic of the poltergeist came up."

"Do you recall who brought up the subject?"

Ginger thought back. "It was Mrs. Richards. I presumed she was only attempting to change the subject from Ambrosia's insensitive comment about the soldiers being too crippled to be choosy over who to dance with, but maybe there was more to it." Ginger shook her head. "I can't imagine any of those women sneaking up on Angela Ashton and stabbing her."

Basil sipped his brandy and stared into space. "Does anyone benefit from Miss Ashton's death?"

"Do you mean financially?"

"I do."

Ginger recalled the Ashtons' humble middle-class family home. "It's hard to say."

"But Miss Ashton could have had a will."

"I suppose, though I wouldn't have guessed her to be the forward-thinking type. Wouldn't you have been notified by now if one existed?"

"Only if a lawyer had been holding it," Basil said. "It's possible one could be hidden away in her house."

"If there is, and Angela Ashton had anything to leave behind, I imagine her mother and sister would stand to benefit."

Basil finished his drink and set the glass on the coffee table. "I believe we should make another visit to Mrs. Ashton and Mrs. Dunsbury in the morning."

CHAPTER 19

The next morning over breakfast, Ginger felt oddly and uncharacteristically shy in front of Basil. Perhaps it was due to the confidences they'd shared whilst rowing on Livingston Lake. She was thankful that Felicia had woken early and joined them.

Mrs. Beasley had cooked them bacon and eggs, and fried haddock, and they washed it down with cups of tea.

Ginger smiled at Felicia who was still in a dull mood. "And whom do we owe for the pleasure of your company so bright and early?"

Felicia brightened a little. "Francis is taking me into St. Albans. He says it will help me take my mind off my troubles. I wanted to go to London, but he said we shouldn't venture too far whilst the . . . situation is still under investigation."

"He's right about that," Basil said. "In fact, I'm not too happy to hear you're leaving Chesterton."

Felicia gasped. "Surely, you don't mean to keep us prisoner in this dreary town? *We* haven't done anything wrong."

"New evidence has come to light, dear," Ginger said. "Hopefully, all shall be cleared up soon."

"New evidence? What have you found out? Do you know who the killer is?"

Basil shot Ginger a look of dismay, and she realised belatedly that she probably shouldn't have said anything to her sister-in-law. But Felicia was so burdened, surely it couldn't hurt to offer her a little hope.

"I'm afraid we're not ready to make an arrest just yet," Basil said. "How long will you and Captain Smithwick be gone?"

"Oh, I don't know. A couple of hours? We're going to do a bit of shopping."

"For what?" Ginger asked sharply. An image of Felicia and Smithwick flashed though her mind.

"He said he'd buy me a new hat," Felicia said with a note of defiance. "Is that a problem?"

Ginger pasted on a smile. "That sounds like fun."

Felicia pushed away from the table. "I know you don't like him, Ginger, but you're just going to have to get used to him being around. And maybe Francis doesn't mean a literal *hat*." She wiggled the fingers of her left hand, underlying Ginger's fears, before storming off.

Basil sipped his tea. "Your sister-in-law is rather sensitive."

"You noticed?" Ginger slumped in her chair, her appetite having disappeared with Felicia. "I don't know what I'll do if she comes home engaged. He's still a suspect!"

"Can I pour you some more tea?" Basil said. "It'll calm you."

Ginger held her floral decorated teacup and matching saucer in the air while Basil poured. "What's on the agenda today?" she asked.

"A second visit to the Ashton family, and then we need to track down the knitting association members."

Ginger sipped her tea, holding the hot cup with two hands, then resting it back on the saucer.

Basil removed his notebook from his suit jacket. "You mentioned Mrs. Richards, a widow; Miss Smith, the volunteer librarian; Miss Whitton who works at the Croft Convalescent Home; and the Honourable Mrs. Croft."

"That's correct."

"The Croft name does tend to come up a lot," Basil said as he returned the notebook to his pocket.

They finished their tea just as Phyllis came to look in on them. "Would you like anything else, madam?" she asked.

"I think we've finished," Ginger said, looking at Basil. He nodded in agreement.

"I would like to drop off our new evidence at the station on the way and get them to send it off to the Yard for fingerprinting and blood analysis," Basil said. "Would you mind if I used your telephone before we go?"

Constable Ryan stood behind the desk in the small brick building that served as the station for law and order in Chesterton.

"Top of the mornin' to ya Lady Gold and Chief Inspector Reed," he said when Ginger and Basil entered.

"Constable Ryan, is Sergeant Maskell available?" Basil asked.

"No sir. The sergeant has taken the next three days off to help his son harvest his cabbages. Can I be of assistance?"

Basil slid the wrapped knitting needle over the counter. "Would you be so kind as to post this to Scotland Yard? I just rang them. They're expecting it."

"A knitting needle?"

"Yes. Be sure not to touch it."

Constable Ryan's dark brow inched upward. "Don't tell me dis is what killed Miss Ashton?"

"It seems likely."

Constable Ryan whistled. "I'll be durned."

"Believe it or not," Basil said. "I've seen stranger things." Turning to Ginger, he added, "After the

Ashtons I'd like to interview the knitting club members. I'm assuming we'll find Miss Whitton and Miss Smith at their respective places of work. And we know where to find the Honourable Mrs. Croft. Do you know where we can find Mrs. Richards?"

Ginger shook her head. "I only just met her myself."

"Quite so," Basil said, remembering. To the constable he asked, "Can I borrow your phone book?"

Constable Ryan handed over the thin volume and Basil flipped through to the R listings.

"Mrs. Doris Richards," Ginger said, looking over his arm.

"Dat would be Mr. Thomas Richards on Church Road," Constable Ryan added, looking happy to help.

Basil jotted the address down and gave the phone book back. "Would you mind drawing us a map?"

Constable Ryan scribbled directions on a piece of notepaper. "Ya cannot miss it. Only just three miles past the old maple tree that got hit by lightning last year. It's black as a berry and broken across the ditch."

"Thank you, Constable," Basil said.

Back in the Austin, Basil and Ginger travelled towards the middle-class area on the outskirts of the village.

Dark, overburdened clouds rumbled in over the hillside. No longer able to bear their heavy load, the clouds unleashed the deluge on the villagers. The wipers on the Austin worked as hard as they could, scraping across the windscreen, but not even their best efforts could clear the view.

Basil pulled over onto the side of the road. "It's best if we wait for the worst to pass."

"I agree," Ginger said. "No sense driving when you can't see the road."

Unlike the Humber, the Austin had a back seat and doors that actually sealed to keep out the wet. Despite this, Ginger felt near to Basil, once again closed in by the weather. She could smell his musky aftershave and see his smooth, freshly shaven face.

She found it difficult to swallow and forced herself to stare out of the passenger window, which to her dismay had fogged up.

Basil kept his eyes straight ahead, seemingly unaffected by their close quarters.

Ginger was quiet for a moment. "I wonder if we'll get snow this year."

"It's a little early."

"But there's a chill in the air."

Basil dipped his chin. "Indeed."

"It often snowed in Boston in October."

"It's almost November."

"So, it could snow soon."

Thankfully the weather system passed as quickly as it came and the sun even dared to stretch out a few long fingers. Basil put the Austin in gear and drove.

The Ashton family home was only ten minutes further on, and he slowed as they approached.

A dog barked and Basil stiffened.

"They didn't have a dog last time."

"Perhaps he came with the children." Ginger pointed to a ball and some wooden blocks left out by the front door.

"Children?"

Ginger cocked her head. "Don't tell me you're afraid of children, too."

"I'm not afraid of children."

"Just dogs."

"Dogs are scary."

Ginger bit the inside of her lip to stop herself from laughing. "I'm sure he's friendly." She stepped out of the car first and the dog proved her a liar. He bared his teeth—white, sharp, and menacing—and let out a warning growl followed by the alarm of deep barking.

Ginger hopped back into the motorcar.

Basil grinned. "I'm not so crazy now, am I?"

"I stand corrected."

The front door of the house cracked open and Mrs. Dunsbury, on seeing Ginger and Basil trapped in their car, whistled at the dog. The animal obediently backed down.

"Hello, Inspector Reed, Lady Gold," she called out. "Don't worry about our mutt. He's all bark and no bite."

Basil muttered under his breath. "Famous last words."

Ginger tentatively stepped out, and Basil followed.

"I'd like to ask you a few more questions." Basil crossed the garden, his eyes darted to the dog at Mrs. Dunsbury's side. "If you don't mind."

"Of course. Do come in." The woman's voice was soft. "I'm speaking quietly because my children are upstairs resting."

Basil removed his hat, and he and Ginger entered the sitting room now occupied by an older woman in a rocking chair. She had long, thin arms clothed in a thin knitted sweater, the cuffs of the sleeves not reaching her wrists. Her hands were mapped with lines and she clutched a handkerchief in one. Salt-and-pepper hair rested in soft curls around a pleasant face. She shared Angela's features, high cheekbones and blue eyes, and despite her weathered skin and frown lines—evidence of a life of hard work—Ginger could see that she'd been beautiful once.

"You must be Mrs. Ashton," Ginger said. "I'm so sorry for your loss."

"Thank you, Lady Gold. I know you've suffered loss yourself and know what it's like."

"I do."

Ginger and Basil claimed the same seats they had when they had last visited. Mrs. Dunsbury offered tea.

"That's quite all right," Basil said. "We're here on police business. Please have a seat."

Worry flashed behind Mrs. Dunsbury's eyes as she slowly lowered herself into the last vacant chair.

Basil began. "Is it possible that Miss Ashton left a will behind?"

Mrs. Dunsbury and Mrs. Ashton shared a quick look, and the elder woman nodded. "Go ahead, Freda."

"As a matter of fact, Inspector," Mrs. Dunsbury said, "she did." Ginger had forgotten about Mrs. Dunsbury's mouth. Her lips twitched, pursing and relaxing, like a pulse.

"And who are the benefactors?" Basil asked.

"I really don't see how this matters," Mrs. Dunsbury said. "It's a private family affair."

"Not when murder is involved," Basil said grimly. "We have to investigate every situation, including who might benefit financially from Miss Ashton's death."

Mrs. Dunsbury paled. "You don't think *I* killed my sister?"

"I'm not here to make accusations," Basil said. "I'm after the facts. Now what are the terms of the will?"

Mrs. Ashton jumped in. "My husband set up a trust for Angela when she became engaged to Mr. Croft." Ginger noted the woman was calm. More so than her eldest daughter. "A dowry of sorts. He passed away before the war ended, and so the trust has remained unaltered."

"What were the terms of the trust?"

"Mr. Ashton invested a small amount—"

Mrs. Dunsbury snorted. "Not small for our sort, Mother. Fifteen pounds!"

"Yes, it was a considerable amount for us, especially in 1914 when war rations were just around the corner. Mr. Ashton invested it in stocks, at Mr. Croft's suggestion. They've done rather well, especially over the last five years."

"How well?" Basil pressed.

"It's now worth three hundred pounds."

Basil whistled. "A goodly sum, indeed. And I gather you are the beneficiary, Mrs. Ashton?"

"No, Inspector," Mrs. Dunsbury said, staring back resolutely. For once her mouth had stilled. "I am."

Basil made a show of looking at his notes. "I made a call to the bank this morning, Mrs. Dunsbury. It appears Mr. Dunsbury had taken out a loan, for your home, wasn't it? Payment in arrears. You were in danger of losing your home, weren't you?"

"We bought it before the war, but since then, well yes, times have been tough. But we were going to pay it. Cecil has been working long hours at the butcher's shop and I've been sewing. You'll see some of my things in the shops in Chesterton."

Basil looked pointedly at Mrs. Dunsbury. "Is it true that Mr. Dunsbury hurt his back at work and was unable to work for a fortnight?"

Lips twitching almost manically. "Yes. Do you know how heavy a side of pork can be?"

Basil ignored the question and asked another of his own. "That trust money will erase your debt problems, won't it?"

"Yes! It's a silver lining to this horrible business."

"Mrs. Dunsbury," Ginger said, cutting in. "Are you acquainted with either Mrs. Thomas Richards or Miss Mary Smith?" Ambrosia had filled in the librarian's Christian name since there was certainly more than one Miss Smith around. "Or Miss Whitton who works as a nurse at the Croft Convalescent Home?" If Freda Dunsbury was complicit in the death of her sister, how was she connected to the knitting association?

Mrs. Dunsbury's eyes darted about the room, to her mother who lifted her chin subtly, and back to Ginger. "Miss Whitton cared for my father before he died. We have no other connection. In fact, I haven't seen her for years."

"I have to ask you this, Mrs. Dunsbury, as a matter of form," Basil said. "Where were you the night of the dance from ten p.m. onwards?"

"I was at home with my children."

"Can someone corroborate that?"

"Well, the children I suppose."

"How old are your children?"

"Clive is eleven, and little Prudence is six."

"Were they not asleep in their beds at that time?"

"Yes, but I wouldn't leave them home alone. Not late at night."

Not even for three hundred pounds? Ginger thought the temptation might be great. Especially since the eldest child was old enough to care for the younger for short periods.

"Where was Mr. Dunsbury?"

"He worked late that night."

"If I hear you right, Mrs. Dunsbury," Basil said, "you don't have a solid alibi."

"I promise you, Inspector," Mrs. Dunsbury said, the muscles around her mouth shifting rapidly. "I didn't kill my sister."

CHAPTER 20

"Freda Dunsbury certainly is the nervous type," Ginger said as she settled back into the Austin.

Basil ignited the engine. "She has motive and opportunity, if one can accept that a woman would leave her children alone to secure the family home and a stable future."

"It's not a stretch to imagine," Ginger said, agreeing. "And she did emphasise the distance between herself and Miss Whitton—almost too much."

"I noticed that. Perhaps Miss Whitton nicked the knitting needle and then gave it to Mrs. Dunsbury who carried out the deed."

"It gives her means, but why go to that kind of trouble to obtain a weapon?"

"To throw the police off the scent," Basil said.

"Muddy the waters. At any rate, it's still all circumstantial. None of it would stand up in court. We must find real evidence of her guilt.

"It begs another question," Ginger added. "What motive does Miss Whitton have?"

"I hope to find that out in due course. But first, let's visit the Richards' residence."

Ginger consulted Constable Ryan's rudimentary map. "Take Blythe Road and turn right onto McMillan Way."

Before they hit the end of the lane, a thick blackened tree with its trunk cracked open appeared as they rounded a bend.

"There it is," Ginger said. "Turn here."

The Austin roared up the drive, announcing their arrival. Though not stately like Bray Manor or Heather's End, the Richards family's three-storey home was imposing in its size.

Mrs. Richards peeked out from behind thick curtains, the lines around her mouth pulling down. Moments later she opened the door before Basil even had a chance to knock.

"Lady Gold," she sputtered. "Had I known you were coming I'd have baked a cake."

"No need to entertain us, Mrs. Richards," Ginger said. "We're here on official police business."

"Oh?" Mrs. Richards said. Chubby fingers played with the ruffled collar of her blouse.

"I'm Chief Inspector Reed from Scotland Yard," Basil said, removing his hat. "Would you mind giving us a moment of your time?"

"Scotland Yard? Oh, dear. All the way from London? Do come in." She motioned for them to follow her. "You must wonder why I answered the door instead of letting my butler get it. I gave him the day off, he had a family emergency. It's so hard to find good staff these days, but—oh, Vera!" The parlour maid skittered into the entrance hall and dipped in a curtsey. "Yes, madam?"

"Bring tea to the drawing room."

The maid bobbed and spun swiftly on her heels as she was bid.

"Is this to do with Miss Angela Ashton?" Mrs. Richards asked. She opened the door to the drawing room and Ginger and Basil followed her in. "I've been to visit her poor mother. Such a dreadful thing, to outlive one's child."

The large room was lavishly decorated with deep, rich wallpaper, long curtains, and plenty of orna-ments and artefacts. A dog's bed lay on the floor by the fireplace. It reminded Ginger of Boss and how she'd left him curled up on the carpet in front of the fireplace in her bedroom.

"Do you have a dog, Mrs. Richards?" she asked.

Mrs. Richards pouted. "Had, I'm afraid. My poor Pal was brutally killed by a reckless driver. Those motorcars are a menace!"

"Oh, I'm sorry." Ginger's heart pinged with empathy. She couldn't even think about what it would be like to lose Boss. "You have a very lovely home," she added, changing the subject.

"Thank you, Lady Gold. I've lived here my whole life. Born and bred in Chesterton."

Ginger studied a large framed picture of a middle-aged man hanging on the wall. "Is this Mr. Richards?"

"Oh, yes. Mr. Richards has been gone for ten years already, but it seems like yesterday."

"Do you have children?"

"Two daughters. My eldest married an American and moved to Minnesota of all places." Her countenance dropped. "I hardly see her. The other still lives with me. Unmarried."

Ginger remembered the yellow cardigan Mrs. Richards was knitting hoping to rectify the situation.

"I have family in America, too," Ginger said. "I do miss my sister awfully."

Mrs. Richards brightened at sharing misery. "Such a shame when families are divided in this way."

Vera arrived with the tea tray, and Ginger was grateful for the refreshment. Mrs. Richards sat in a comfortable-looking chair, similar to the one Ambrosia made claim to. She and Basil sat on the settee on the other side of the tea table.

"Any word on when the funeral will be?" Mrs. Richards asked.

"Sometime after the inquest," Basil said.

Mrs. Richards propped her teacup and saucer on her lap. "So, what can I do to help?"

"We're actually here to enquire about the alleged poltergeist at Bray Manor," Basil said.

Mrs. Richards' small eyes flashed with amusement. "Is Scotland Yard now investigating the supernatural?"

"A missing item has been tied to the murder investigation. Do you know who's behind the pranks?"

"You mean to say you think someone has deliberately moved items in Bray Manor? I just assumed the Dowager Lady Gold was growing forgetful."

"We have reason to believe that Dowager Lady Gold's concerns have merit," Basil said.

"I know it's hard to imagine," Ginger said, "but do you think anyone in the knitting circle could be behind this?"

"Well, I don't rightly know." Mrs. Richards pushed up on her spectacles. "If I had to guess, I'd say Miss Smith."

"Why Miss Smith?" Basil asked.

Mrs. Richards' beady eyes grew even smaller. "She's a spinster with nothing of merit to do. Yes, she volunteers at our little library, but really, can anything be duller? I know I'd go batty with boredom if I were her." Mrs. Richard's chuckled. "She might've been after a bit of harmless fun."

Ginger let her irritation show. "My grandmother doesn't find it funny."

"Oh, yes," Mrs. Richard's expression grew dour, and she brushed imaginary fluff off her wool skirt. "My apologies, madam. Miss Smith should be stopped at once."

fter saying their goodbyes to Mrs. Richards, Ginger and Basil went directly to the library to call on Miss Mary Smith. The Chesterton village library was one open room with a children's section in one corner and an office to the right of the front desk. Miss Smith was positioned behind the desk, her spectacles perched on her nose and a novel propped up in one hand. She blinked in surprise to see the inspector and Ginger walking towards her. Miss Smith opened a drawer and quickly dropped the book in.

"Lady Gold! How marvellous to see you." She stood and cupped her hands. "Are you looking for a book? What genre do you like?"

"I'm a mystery detective reader myself," Ginger said.

"Ah, a fan of Sherlock Holmes, I bet. Unfortunately, all the copies we have are signed out, but have you heard of Agatha Christie? She's new to crime writing and all the rage. There's still a copy of her latest book on the shelf."

Ginger nodded. "I have heard of her, and I've read all her books. But that's not why we're here." She motioned to Basil. "This is Chief Inspector Reed from Scotland Yard."

"Ohhh. . ." Miss Smith let the word roll out. "I heard about that horrid affair after the dance. Couldn't believe it. Poor Miss Ashton. Such a pleasant girl."

Ginger was always surprised where the line between Miss Ashton's friends and enemies lay.

Miss Smith continued, "And so horrible for you Lady Gold! Such an awful tragedy occurring at Bray Manor."

"Yes," Ginger admitted. "It's quite awful."

"I'd like to ask you a few questions if I may?" Basil said.

Miss Smith's eyes darted to the young mother who had just entered. She nodded at Miss Smith in greeting and shepherded her two young sons to the children's corner. Miss Smith waved towards the office behind her. "In here, please, where it's more private."

Ginger held back as Basil followed Miss Smith. Curious about the book Miss Smith was so keen on hiding, Ginger slid open the desk drawer. Interesting. The good librarian wasn't stretching her intellect with literary fiction, but with nineteenth-century rubbish known as a shilling shocker.

Under it was a set of four pencils tied together in a "T", an apparatus used for shooting elastic bands and small pencils. A piece of paper hung on the wall perpendicular to the desk with a rudimentary bull's eye drawn on. Mrs. Richards was right about Miss Smith's boredom. If it were Ginger, she'd have shot those loose elastic bands across the room a thousand times.

On the desk, there was a notepad with sketches of flowers, birds and nature scenes. Miss Smith had talent and Ginger thought that perhaps the volunteer hours spent at the library were misused.

Basil paused at the office door and cleared his throat. Ginger surreptitiously closed the desk drawer and hurried inside.

"Miss Smith, please don't be alarmed," Ginger said. "We're simply trying to get to the bottom of this poltergeist problem before my grandmother's nerves are the end of her."

Miss Smith pushed her spectacles up on the bridge of her nose. "Oh. I hope you settle things, Lady Gold. I do adore your grandmother, and this kind of trick is so unkind."

Ginger recalled the suppressed giggle Miss Smith had expressed on the night of the knitting circle but said nothing. After all, one could find something funny in the moment without wishing harm. Like when someone trips and falls, for instance. Laughter is spontaneous even while concern for the person's well-being is authentic.

"Is there anyone in the knitting circle you think might be tempted to play poltergeist on the Dowager Lady Gold?" Ginger asked.

"Oh, my." Miss Smith's shoulders slumped forward as she nibbled on her bottom lip. "I feel like I'm being asked to tattle on my friends at school."

Basil leaned forward. "Miss Smith, we have reason to believe that finding the poltergeist will help us to solve Miss Ashton's murder."

Miss Smith's eyes grew round, exaggerated by the lenses, reminding Ginger of the animated cartoon, *Felix the Cat*.

"I do hate to gossip." Miss Smith said, "But if that's the case then, I'll tell you. Mrs. Richards didn't take her loss at the Summer Bloom festival to the Dowager Lady Gold lightly. She claims she had the best roses, but that the judges were soft on Dowager Lady Gold because of her title. And as for poor Miss Ashton, I don't think Mrs. Richards could ever forgive her for running over her dog, but I'm certain she wouldn't have killed over it."

Ginger and Basil shared a quick look. Mrs. Richards had failed to mention the connection between losing her dog and the murder victim.

It was interesting that Mrs. Richards pointed to Miss Smith and Miss Smith pointed back. Ginger was about to ask what her friendship to Mrs. Richards was like when the librarian spoke again.

"But then there's the Honourable Mrs. Croft. You know how the uppers are with their titles and positions—no offence to you Lady Gold—but Dowager Lady Gold has a way of keeping Mrs. Croft in her place, you know, without having to say a word. Just the way the dowager carries herself and how she speaks down to others. Again, I wouldn't be so forward if it weren't for the urgency of the situation. And the Honourable Mrs. Croft was so worried about her son. Miss Ashton was a badge of humiliation for the poor woman. Just rotten luck."

"You know a lot about your association members," Basil said.

Miss Smith blushed. "I overhear a lot in the library, Chief Inspector. You're not supposed to talk, but people do. They whisper, of course, but I can still hear them."

"What about Miss Whitton?" Basil asked. "Any reason she might play a game with the Dowager Lady Gold?"

"Hmm," Miss Smith said, slowing down as if she was finally stumped. "I honestly can't imagine Miss Whitton doing such a thing. But she does dote on her younger brother—he's only seventeen you know, but quite fetching. Girls of *all* ages have been eyeing him. Miss Ashton, for example, was at least seven years his senior, and Miss Whitton took issue with how Miss Ashton flirted with the boy."

If Miss Whitton's maternal instincts for her brother were anything like Ginger's feelings for Felicia, then Ginger could understand how strong the urge to protect one's own could be.

CHAPTER 22

*M*iss Whitton was on duty at the Croft Convalescent Home. She looked serious in her white uniform and nurse's cap as she pushed a soldier in a wheelchair down the hall.

"Miss Whitton?" Ginger called out as they approached. Like the other knitting circle members, she regarded them with surprise.

"Lady Gold?"

"Could you spare a moment of your time? It's important."

The soldier eyed Ginger and Basil, then looked to Miss Whitton. "It's fine, Sister," he said. "I can make it to the games room from here."

The man grabbed onto the large wheels of his wooden chair and pushed down the hall, the small, third wheel at the back creaking.

"Miss Whitton," Ginger said when the soldier had

turned the corner. "This is Chief Inspector Reed from Scotland Yard here to investigate the death of Miss Angela Ashton."

Miss Whitton blinked. "I see. Hello."

The ward was bustling with nurses walking quickly, former soldiers moving about, some playing games like chess and cards. Others just sat, staring out of the window into the courtyard.

"Is there somewhere we can talk in private?" Basil asked.

"It's fairly busy here as you can see," Miss Whitton said. "But I believe one of the visitors' rooms is vacant." Miss Whitton opened the door to a small room with comfortable chairs circling a table.

"Would you like some tea or coffee?" she offered.

"That's quite all right," Basil said. "We shan't be long."

The nurse lowered herself into a chair, as Ginger and Basil claimed seats across from her.

"Very well," Miss Whitton said.

"Miss Whitton, do you suspect anyone in your knitting circle who may be responsible for the poltergeist affair?" Basil asked.

Miss Whitton hesitated. "I *don't* suspect. I know."

"You *know* who's been playing this game with my grandmother?"

"I do, Lady Gold, but it was difficult for me to interfere. I was rather in a tight spot."

"Are you suggesting Mrs. Croft is at fault?" Ginger

asked. As an employee at the Croft Convalescent Home, that would put Miss Whitton in an uncomfortable position.

Miss Whitton confirmed by nodding her head. "I caught her red-handed. She stared back at me, horrified. I quickly busied myself, pretending I hadn't seen her. We've never mentioned it. I figured she'd tire of the game and would eventually stop."

With Mrs. Croft's height and build, she could have moved the heavy coat rack on her own.

"To your knowledge did Mrs. Croft take anything from the sitting room when she left Bray Manor the night of the last knitting meeting?" Basil asked.

Miss Whitton's mouth tightened and she breathed out sharply through her nose.

"Might I remind you, Miss Whitton," Basil said, "that this is a murder investigation."

Miss Whitton sighed. "I do hope this doesn't come back to haunt me, no pun intended, but yes. Mrs. Croft took a knitting needle belonging to Miss Gold."

So now they knew the identity of the poltergeist, Ginger thought, but did that make Mrs. Croft a killer? Things certainly didn't look good for her.

"I understand you and Miss Ashton weren't friends," Basil stated.

"Why would we be friends?" Miss Whitton said with contempt. "She's younger and runs in a different circle."

"We understand you have a brother," Basil returned. "Mr. James Whitton."

Miss Whitton's mouth dropped open at the sudden change of subject. "I do, but I don't see what he has to do with anything."

"We've learned that Miss Ashton fancied him."

"All the girls fancy James, Inspector."

"So it didn't bother you that an older, engaged woman was showing interest?"

"Of course it bothered me. Angela Ashton was a tart! Had she met you, Inspector, I'm sure you would've been a prospect as well. The woman was insatiable."

Ginger watched for Basil's reaction to Miss Whitton's short outburst, admiring how he remained professional and unruffled. At least Miss Whitton had the decency to blush.

"My brother looks like a man, but he's still a boy —only seventeen. A foolish dalliance with any woman could ruin his life." Her eyes brightened with pride. "He's going to university."

"You'd do anything to protect him, wouldn't you?" Basil said.

The nurse stared hard at Basil, not answering the question. "I have an alibi. I was at home with my brother all evening. He lives with me, you see. He was home at the weekend."

"Can anyone else verify this?" Basil asked.

"Is James' word not enough?"

Basil didn't answer.

"Fine. Perhaps my neighbour noticed. I really can't say. I hate to mention this, with you present, Lady Gold, but don't dismiss the possibility of Miss Felicia Gold's involvement just because of her status and relationship to you."

Ginger swallowed. Something about her sister-in-law's behaviour had niggled at the back of Ginger's mind, but she had dutifully pushed it away. "What do you mean?"

"You've met Miss Gold's gentleman? The debonair Captain Smithwick?" Miss Whitton said with an uncharitable glint in her eye. "Miss Gold's quite possessive, you know. My brother wasn't the only man to catch Miss Ashton's attention."

CHAPTER 23

The annoyance Ginger had felt at Miss Whitton's insinuation had brewed to anger by the time she got back to Basil's car. To cast suspicion on Felicia like that! Surely, a sign of desperation. Ginger closed the door of the Austin a little harder than necessary.

Basil shot her a look.

Ginger sat up straight, her lips pursed together. "A sibling alibi isn't the strongest of sorts."

Basil merely hummed as he started the engine.

"Let's surmise for a moment that Miss Whitton did take it," Basil said as he put the motorcar into gear. "She's very protective of her brother and would do anything to guard his welfare—which is motive. If she took the knitting needle she had means, but what of opportunity? Did she plan in advance to kill Miss

Ashton on Saturday night? Am I correct that she wasn't at the dance?"

"You are. But that doesn't mean she wasn't waiting outside. She might've guessed that Miss Ashton would venture out eventually."

"It's possible," Basil admitted. "But surely there would be a better time and opportunity. With so many people about, she might've been spotted."

"Actually, the dance is a great cover. Look at all the potential suspects it's provided."

Basil conceded. "True. But Mrs. Croft still has the better motive. If she took the knitting needle, she'd have means. She was at the dance, which gave her opportunity. And we're already aware of her motive."

Ginger shook her head. "I just can't picture it. Stabbing is so vulgar, more of a man's *modus operandi*, than a society woman's."

"Murderers come in all shapes and sizes, Ginger. You can trust me on that. And women have been known to stab people to death."

Ginger's lips pulled upward and a sense of warmth spread across her chest. She realised that she did trust him.

"Shall we visit the Croft family first?" Basil asked. Ginger's heart dropped. She knew what he meant by "first." Felicia was now firmly on the suspect list. Ginger simply nodded.

Basil pulled into the long drive that led to the Croft family mansion.

"Won't they be surprised to see us again so soon," Ginger said.

"Or maybe they won't be surprised," Basil countered.

The stalwart butler answered the chimes of the doorbell and repeated his mantra. "The Croft family isn't taking visitors."

"This is a police matter," Basil said. "Please let the Honourable Mrs. Croft know Chief Inspector Reed from Scotland Yard is here."

Moments later, the butler showed Ginger and Basil into the drawing room where an anxious Mrs. Croft sat in the same wingback chair and Patrick Croft puffed on his pipe as he sat, legs crossed in a chair next to the fireplace. Today he wore a more serious outfit, a dark double-breasted suit and glossy patent leather shoes with shiny gold toecaps.

"Another visit?" Patrick said on seeing them. "To what do we owe the honour?"

"We just have a few questions for Mrs. Croft," Ginger said. Then to the woman, "About the knitting association."

Mrs. Croft's fingers clutched at the smooth wooden armrests. "The knitting association?"

"We're trying to get to the bottom of the poltergeist affair," Ginger said.

Mr. Croft laughed. "The Yard's put one of their men on the ghost? What next?"

"I did it!" Mrs. Croft shouted.

"Mother!"

"I'm ashamed, but I can't bear the burden of my crime any longer."

"Your crime?" Basil said.

"Yes, yes. Oh, dear Lord, *I'm* the poltergeist!"

Miss Whitton had told the truth. Ginger shook her head. "But, why Mrs. Croft? I don't understand."

"Oh, I know it's shameful, Lady Gold, please don't judge me too harshly, but your grandmother really gets my goat. Always looking down her nose and with a snide remark at the ready. I only wanted to bring her down a few pegs."

Miss Smith's assessment about the friction between the Dowager Lady Gold and Mrs. Croft had been correct.

"Did you take Miss Gold's knitting needle?" Basil asked. "One of the ones with the pearl ends?"

"I did, oh . . . I feel so humiliated! I slipped it into my knitting basket and was going to hide it in the umbrella stand as I left. I set my basket on the bench in the entrance hall to gather my coat, and when I later searched for it, the needle was gone. I thought it had fallen out. I didn't stay around to find out where; I just hoped a maid would discover it and return it to Miss Gold."

She stared up at Ginger with sad, watery eyes.

"Oh, Lady Gold, I am very sorry."

"Would it shock you to know that the missing knitting needle was the weapon used to kill Miss Ashton?" Basil said.

Mrs. Croft let out a cry and her son choked on his pipe. "Steady on, Inspector," he said. "You can't be serious."

"Dead serious. Forgive the pun."

Mrs. Croft moaned. "Patrick, dear, I feel faint."

"I'll fetch some smelling salts, Mummy. Hold on tight."

Mrs. Croft held a lace handkerchief to her nose and blew. "I knew what I was doing was childish, but I just couldn't help myself. I had no idea it would lead to this." She stared at Basil, pleading. "I didn't hurt that girl, I promise. I didn't like her, but I would never do something as gruesome as that."

A maid hurried in with the smelling salts, and Mrs. Croft waved her away. "I'm fine now. Leave us." The maid left just as Patrick Croft returned.

"Surely, you can't believe my mother had anything to do with the demise of Miss Ashton?"

"Mr. Croft," Basil began, "where were you from midnight to one o'clock in the early hours of Sunday the twenty-eighth?"

"He was with me," Mrs. Croft said. "We were on our way home. You can ask our driver."

"I'll do that," Basil said. "In the meantime, Mrs. Croft, I'm charging you with mischief."

"What? You can't put me in prison." Her full face turned red as a tomato. "I'd never survive prison!"

"It's okay, Mrs. Croft," Basil said. "It won't come to that. So long as you stay in Chesterton. There may be a fine, that's all. It depends on whether or not Dowager Lady Gold presses charges."

Mrs. Croft moaned again and slid lower in her chair. "Patrick, I think I'll need those salts after all."

CHAPTER 24

"My intuition says Mrs. Croft didn't kill Angela Ashton, but I'm still annoyed at her for playing those hurtful tricks on Ambrosia."

Basil smirked. "Who does your *intuition* say it is?"

Ginger wrinkled her nose at Basil. Her instincts were letting her down. At times all the suspects were guilty, and at other times, none of them were. "I'm still working it out," she finally said. "Who do *you* think killed her?"

"Unfortunately I can't go by intuition," Basil said as he drummed his thumbs on the steering wheel. "I can only go by the facts."

"Okay. What are the *facts* telling you?"

"Mr. Croft is the most likely culprit. He's making light of it, but the truth is he's now out of an unfortunate situation."

"He's also out of the dowry—the trust Mr. Ashton set up."

"I hardly think he's in need of money."

"Oh, you'd be surprised at how 'poor' a lot of the rich are."

Basil suggested they stop for refreshments, and Ginger agreed. With the way this case was going, she wouldn't mind a drink right about now.

"There's the White Stag," she suggested. "On Rose Lane."

"I remember it," Basil said.

Basil steered the motorcar through town. The streets were cobbled, and Ginger held on as they bounced over several deep potholes. Though small, Chesterton was a lively village, with street merchants selling their autumn harvests of marrows, carrots, and potatoes. They passed motorists, but also a good number of horses pulling carts of hay and other wares. A young boy ran in front of them as he chased a chicken and Basil stomped on the brake.

Ginger held onto her hat and blurted, "This town is a throwback in time. I often wonder if the citizens here are still saluting the queen."

Basil shouted at the boy and, once the coast was clear, drove slowly forward.

Ginger moved her focus from the boy to the pedestrians walking along the pavement. She almost missed seeing Felicia, hand in hand with Captain Smithwick as they turned down a lane.

"There's Felicia," she said, pointing. "Go after her." She softened her bossy tone by adding, "If you don't mind."

Basil indicated and turned right, driving slowly up behind Smithwick and Felicia who was staring up at the captain adoringly. Basil brought the Austin to a stop and softly honked the horn announcing their presence. Ginger removed herself from the vehicle, pasted a smile on her face and approached.

"Felicia, darling. I thought it was you. Weren't you off to St. Albans today?"

Felicia held onto Smithwick's arm. "We've been and returned. We were just going to have a meal at the Chesterton Inn. It's very quaint, I think, don't you, Ginger?"

"Very." Ginger's gaze moved to Felicia's left hand. Though she wore gloves, there was no tell-tale bump indicating a new piece of jewellery. Ginger wasn't surprised. Smithwick wasn't the type of man to tie himself down, not even in service of the king. Felicia's eyes followed Ginger's gaze and pulled her left hand out of view. Though Felicia's lips remained in a smile, Ginger could sense her sister-in-law's disappointment.

Ginger locked eyes with Smithwick deftly transmitting her disapproval. The corner of his mouth inched up in victory.

Felicia noted the exchange. "What is going on between you two?" she demanded.

"Nothing, dear," Ginger said. "It's all water under

the bridge. Why don't you come home with us now, and save Captain Smithwick a trip."

Felicia scoffed. "I'm not going home now. I just told you we're going to the Chesterton Inn. Francis is buying me dinner. I'd invite you and the inspector, but it's meant to be romantic."

It all happened quickly: The strap of Ginger's handbag slipped off her shoulder; she lifted her arm to catch it. Captain Smithwick mistook her action, believing she would slap him and he caught her by the wrist and held tight.

"Let me go," Ginger hissed.

Before Smithwick could comply, Basil appeared from behind her, fist first, and let a right hook fly.

Felicia screamed.

Smithwick stumbled back but kept his balance. "You just hit a senior officer, Lieutenant," he snarled.

Ginger recalled Basil saying they'd served in the same regiment for a short while.

"The war is over, *Captain*," Basil said. "In today's world, I outrank you."

Smithwick made to leave, then pivoted back sharply, diving into Basil. He wrapped his arms around the inspector's waist and rammed him into a gaslight. Basil twisted, forcing them both to slam up against the outside wall of a hair salon. The window filled with a well-dressed stylist and two women having their hair marcelled. The ruckus had drawn a crowd.

"—such an unruly disturbance!"

"Outsiders."

"Foreigners, likely."

Someone shouted for the attention of a police officer on the beat.

Basil found himself with his back against the wall, a victim to Smithwick's fists. First to the face, then to the abdomen. Basil let out a cry of pain.

A pistol shot into the air.

The men froze. A woman screamed.

"A revolver!"

"Must be Americans!"

"I told ya they was foreigners!"

Smithwick turned, his determined eyes set on the weapon in Ginger's hand pointed directly at him.

"Nice piece," he said. "Do you always carry?"

"Only when I think I might run into you. Now step away from the inspector."

Smithwick slowly raised his hands and shuffled back. "Is that thing even licensed?"

"Will it matter when you're dead?"

Smithwick laughed.

"I may not have fought with weapons during the war." Mostly. "But I grew up in America where children learned how to shoot."

"Right," Smithwick said. "I've heard about the Wild West."

"Ginger," Felicia said, her voice quavering. "Put the gun away."

Ginger lowered the small Remington Derringer and slipped it back into her handbag just as Constable Ryan sprinted around the corner. "Lady Gold?" he said with surprise.

"Hello, Constable. So sorry to have disturbed you."

"A gunshot was reported."

Ginger shook her head and leaned in close to the constable so others wouldn't hear. "These gentlemen were working out a disagreement. I'm afraid someone heard a motorcar backfiring and let their imagination run away on them."

Constable Ryan took in the scene: Felicia pale as a bleached sheet, Captain Smithwick straightening his tie, Inspector Basil roughed up and on the pavement."

"Inspector!" Constable Ryan rushed to his side.

"I'm fine, Ryan," Basil mumbled, looking embarrassed. "Continue on."

Constable Ryan took a hesitant step back. "Are ya certain?"

"Yes. Just, clear the crowd."

The constable took his task seriously and soon the lane was cleared, leaving Ginger and Felicia alone with Smithwick and Basil.

Ginger ran to the inspector's side. "Basil?" Blood leaked from his nose and black was already forming around his eyes. "Can you get up?"

"War injury," he said with difficulty. His arms wrapped possessively around his abdomen.

Ginger stared at Felicia. "Darling, you can either walk away with Smithwick or help me get Inspector Reed back to Bray Manor. The choice is yours, but the captain is leaving."

It was a bluff. There was no way in hades she was letting Felicia leave with Smithwick, but she knew her sister-in-law, and things would go a lot better if the decision was hers. Ginger's bluff paid off.

No longer haughty, Felicia was clearly shaken by the altercation, her eyes reflecting her disappointment. The romantic mood was broken. "Francis, don't be angry, but I'm going to go home now."

Smithwick picked up his hat, placed it firmly on his head, and tipped it towards Ginger. "You've won this round, Lady Gold." His shoulders snapped back as he marched away, forever a soldier.

Ginger snarled. If she never saw the blighter again, it would be too soon. She turned her attention back to Basil. "Put your weight on me," she instructed. "Felicia, get his other side."

Together they helped Basil into the backseat of his motorcar. The keys were still in the ignition and Ginger started it up. "I'm taking you to the surgery," she called over her shoulder.

"No," Basil said, leaning heavily against the door. "Just take me to Bray Manor. I'll be fine after a rest."

Ginger hated to do it, but she acquiesced. There wasn't much a doctor could do for a bloody nose, though the abdominal injury was worrying.

181

They were quiet on the drive home. Ginger's gaze volleyed from the road in front, to Basil in her rear view mirror, to Felicia who stared despondently out of the window.

"Are you all right, Felicia?"

Felicia turned to look at her. "Francis said you'd won this round. What did he mean by that?"

"Darling, it's all buried along with the war dead. Is it enough for me to tell you that he's not what you think he is?"

Felicia's shoulders began to quiver and Ginger dared to take one hand off the broad steering wheel to dig through her handbag for a handkerchief. She held it out for Felicia who accepted it and held it to her face as she softly sobbed. Finally she spoke again, her words sounding choked and squeaky. "I thought you were jealous of me. Can you imagine that? And all along Francis was using me to get to you."

"He doesn't want me, at least not like that."

"Then like how?"

Ginger sighed. "There's something he wants me to do for him. But I refused. Our Captain Smithwick is the type of man who's used to getting his way. When he doesn't, he stoops to all sorts of childish ploys."

"Well, I've finished with him," Felicia said. She sat up straight and crossed her arms in defiance. "Even if I become an old spinster. No one uses Felicia Gold."

Ginger smiled at her with pride. "Now, that's my girl."

CHAPTER 25

*a*fter instructing Felicia to fetch Wilson, Ginger turned in her seat to study Basil. Propped up against the back window, he held a bloodied handkerchief to his nose. Telling herself she was feeling compassion for a friend, she wanted to reach over to grab his hand and comfort him.

Or did she feel something deeper? She quickly pushed that idea aside and kept her hands to herself.

"How are you feeling, Inspector?"

He inhaled through his mouth and winced. "I think my nose has stopped bleeding."

"I should be angry with you," Ginger said.

"Why?"

"For punching the captain like that. It was uncalled for."

"But he was manhandling you!"

Ginger's heart warmed at Basil's emphatic need to defend her.

"He wasn't hurting me. Besides, I can take care of myself and Smithwick knew it. Instead you made a dreadful scene and now look at you."

Basil scowled at the chastisement.

Ginger knew Smithwick could do a lot worse in a shorter amount of time, and that he'd held back. Otherwise, Basil would be dead. The captain was showing off or making a point. Or both.

"Well, I'll thank you anyway," Ginger said. "Smithwick is a brute. I just wish it were he that had a pair of black eyes to show for it, not you."

"As do I, Lady Gold," Basil mumbled. He opened the door and Ginger stopped him.

"Wilson is on his way, see there, he's at the door."

"It's okay. I can walk." Basil took a step and swooned. Ginger stepped out at once and caught him just in time.

"You might be concussed," she said. "You hit your head on that brick wall pretty hard."

Wilson moved like a hurrying penguin and ducked to take on Basil's weight. "Where to, madam?"

"I don't think he's ready for the stairs. Let's put him on the couch in the telephone room until he regains his strength."

It was a slow journey. At least the leather couch was six feet long so Basil could stretch out.

"Felicia, be a brick and bring the inspector some

water." Ginger could've called for a maid, or assigned the task to Wilson, but she felt her sister-in-law was in need of something to do.

Wilson left and returned shortly with a damp cloth.

"You can leave us now, Wilson. I'll tend to the inspector."

Ginger removed her coat, hat, and gloves and draped them over a chair. Pulling the ottoman up to the couch she sat, using the dampened cloth to gently work away the blood from the inspector's face. He kept his eyes closed and though he winced at the tender points, Ginger sensed that he enjoyed the procedure, too.

"Too bad Haley isn't here," she said. "She'd be a better nurse to you."

Basil's lip curled up on one side. "I'm quite content with you."

The way he said it, a sanguine whisper, made Ginger's heart skip a beat. She quickly reprimanded herself. *Be professional!*

Basil's hand rested over his abdomen. Ginger had caught him favouring his lower left side in the past.

"What kind of injury did you sustain in the war?"

"Gun shot. Lost my spleen and almost my life, but for a miracle I can't explain."

"France?"

"First battle of Ypres. I'm afraid I didn't last long. Turns out I wasn't much good at soldiering. My commanders determined I was no longer fit for the front and needed to engage in an essential homeland occupation."

Ginger hummed. "That's why you joined the Metropolitan Police Force?"

Basil watched her through swollen eyes. "Yes. If I couldn't serve Britain on the battlefield abroad, then I could damn well serve her at home. I had to preserve my dignity somehow."

"Weren't you tempted to leave the force when the war ended?" Ginger knew Basil didn't need to work since his family was monied. She would never admit it to Basil, but she had looked into his past the last time their paths had crossed.

"I thought I would be," Basil said. "But in the end, I found I quite liked it. Working at the Yard gives me a reason to get up in the morning and a sense of satisfaction when I go to bed at night."

"I take it your wife wasn't as enthusiastic." Ginger felt at liberty to ask such a personal question since Basil had offered word of his divorce freely.

"Policing is a demanding taskmaster. It takes a man's time and suppresses his emotions. Emelia wanted more than I could give on both fronts and found someone else who could."

Ginger had suspected adultery, as the courts weren't gracious about granting divorces on other counts.

"Were you happy together once?" Ginger asked

softly, knowing she had crossed the line into something very familiar, something a mere acquaintance would never ask. "Before the war?"

Basil sighed, and for a moment Ginger feared he wouldn't answer her. She quickly added, "I'm sorry. That's too personal. I shouldn't have asked."

"It's okay, Ginger." His hand rested on hers.

Shots of electricity raced through her being. She stilled, not wanting to break the spell.

"I thought we were happy, but now I'm not so sure."

Ginger felt sad for the inspector. She, at least, could be thankful to have experienced deep love and true happiness in her life, even if short-lived.

Basil shifted, his hand moving from Ginger to his side, and winced.

"Are you in much pain?" Ginger asked. "I can track down some aspirin."

"I would like that. Thank you."

Felicia finally arrived with the requested water, and Ginger immediately sent her to fetch aspirin. She helped Basil raise his head to sip from the glass. The telephone rang causing them both to startle, and Basil grimaced with the suddenness of his movement. Ginger quickly answered it.

"Bray Manor, Lady Gold speaking."

She handed the candlestick apparatus to Basil and said, "It's Scotland Yard."

Remaining prostrate, Basil held the receiver to his ear.

"Reed here."

The call was short, and Basil handed the receiver back. He looked at Ginger, regret flashing behind his bruised eyes. "The report on the knitting needle came in. Only Felicia's prints on it. Blood traces match Miss Ashton's blood." He pushed up on his elbows, his eyes pinching closed at the pain.

Then he held Ginger's gaze. "Felicia had motive, means, and opportunity. I'm sorry, I have to take her in."

CHAPTER 26

Ginger gaped at Basil. She studied his face, searching for a hint of a smile. "You're not serious. The knitting needle belonged to Felicia. Of course her prints would be on it!" Ginger wished Mrs. Croft's prints had been found—it would've diluted the evidence, but a culture of glove-wearing had eliminated that possibility.

Basil wrestled up into a full sitting position and swung his feet to the floor with a groan. Ginger no longer felt sorry for him and in no way helped him to his feet. Basil ran fingers through his oiled hair, smoothing it into position, then wiped his hand on his handkerchief. He folded the square piece of cotton and slipped it back into his breast pocket.

"It's not personal, Ginger, and I'm sorry to have to do it, but it's my obligation. Please summon her for me."

Ginger glared at him, finding his request inconceivable. When Ginger failed to move, Basil hobbled out of the telephone room in search of Felicia himself.

Ginger stayed hot on his heels. "You will *not* go upstairs."

He held his side and squinted at her through swollen eyes. "I do believe that my personal belongings are up there."

Ginger followed as Basil slowly pulled himself upward, hand steady on the banister. "You will not go to Felicia's room."

"Ginger. I need to take her in for questioning."

"You can question her here."

"That's not how the Met works."

"We're not in London!"

Ginger struggled with her rising emotion. If she wanted Basil to allow her to assist with his investigation, she had to be willing to go where the evidence led. But Felicia? A maternal-type protective instinct enveloped her with surprising ferociousness.

Basil stilled on the landing. "I'm sorry, Ginger, I truly am. After that phone call with my superintendent, my hands are tied."

Phyllis crossed the passage in front of them, her arms carrying a large pile of folded linens. Basil called out. "Miss Howard!"

The maid stopped in her tracks and then approached. "Can I help you, Inspector?"

"Please summon Miss Gold for me."

Ginger stared hard at the maid. "Do not, Phyllis. Continue on."

Basil shook his head then held his hand to his temple. Ginger hoped it hurt.

"Felicia isn't a killer," she said through gritted teeth. "If you arrest her, the real murderer will get away. This farce is a waste of time."

Phyllis crossed the passage again, this time with empty arms. She risked a curious glance their way before staring hard at the floor.

"Miss Howard," Basil called again.

The maid's thin lips pulled down as her eyes darted anxiously from the inspector to Ginger and back, her loyalty to the Gold family in conflict with the authority of the inspector.

Basil sighed. "This is a murder investigation. Miss Howard, please let Miss Gold know I need to see her in the entrance hall."

Ginger huffed. "At least let me prepare her. Would you take her into custody without proper notice?"

Ginger stormed down the passage to Felicia's room, hesitating briefly before knocking. A sideways glance proved that the insufferable inspector had remained in his place, watching her. Rage pricked hotly under her skin. This was absurd! And scandalous! Ginger had never worried about what it would mean to taint the family name before, but now that she was back in England, she understood how damaging and life-changing it could be. Felicia's reputation would be ruined.

"Felicia darling, it's me."

Felicia beckoned her inside.

"Is something the matter?" Felicia asked, concern crossing her youthful face. "You look as if you've seen a ghost." She frowned. "Don't tell me we've got another poltergeist."

Felicia wore a three-quarter-length dressing gown with playful ruffles around the cap sleeves, collar, and down the middle surrounding a string of buttons. She looked younger than her twenty-one years, and Ginger was reminded of the first time she'd met her —a precocious eleven-year-old, dearly smitten with her older brother, and not wanting to share his affections with his new bride in any way. The early days of Ginger's visits to Bray Manor were spent in a battle of the wills with the child, but Ginger had experience dealing with her own headstrong younger sister, and Felicia soon discovered that her antics did not sway or dismantle Ginger's confidence.

Ginger knew the only way a child's tantrums produced the desired effect was if the child had an audience to witness them. Ginger would smile at Felicia and find reason to ignore her. Soon little Felicia was vying for *Ginger's* attention, not Daniel's, and Ginger was quick to give her the love and maternal affection the motherless child had longed for.

Felicia's room—dotted with sentimental dolls and

remnants from her younger years—reflected her shielded childhood. Not from heartache—the war held no prejudices when it came to that—but from poverty and want. Despite Felicia's emotional distress at having her eyes opened to Smithwick's dark side, she had little experience with real hardship. Even her days working as a land girl in the war were served caring for animals on a farm. Hard and dirty physical work compared to how Felicia now spent her days, but not anything that would break the girl's spirit. Fear gripped Ginger's heart. This situation was very different. She swallowed the dry lump that had formed in her throat.

"Felicia, darling, I have some distressing news."

Felicia wrinkled her nose. "Oh dear, what now?"

"The pathology results from the knitting needle are in. There are traces of Angela's blood on it."

"Oh, my!" Felicia's shoulder's folded in with the weight of the news. "Someone used *my* knitting needle to kill her?"

"They only found your fingerprints on it."

"Of course my fingerprints would be on it."

"That's what I said."

Felicia held Ginger's gaze with an unnerving intensity. "I sense a 'but.'"

Ginger sat on the bed beside Felicia and took her hand. "Darling, I'm afraid the Yard has set their eyes on you. In their mind, you had means, opportunity and motive. Inspector Reed is waiting in the passage to take you into custody for questioning."

Felicia's eyelashes batted wildly. "I don't understand. He can't think I—"

"Of course not! No one does. He's only following protocol. I'll get you the best solicitor—"

"Am I being arrested? For *murder*?" Felicia burst into tears. "Oh Ginger!"

Felicia's hot tears stirred Ginger's anger. Such inane injustice. She couldn't believe Basil Reed would arrest her sister-in-law with hardly a shred of real evidence. It was all purely circumstantial!

She thought she and Basil were friends, but this, *this* was the worst betrayal. Curse Scotland Yard for forcing his hand!

"Ginger, I'll never be able to show my face in public again. My reputation shall never recover!" Felicia's eyes registered the worst possibility. "They might *hang* me!"

"No one is going to hang you," Ginger said. Not over her dead body. She held Felicia, rubbing her back as the girl sobbed. "Now, now," Ginger said soothingly. "Wipe your tears and stand tall. We'll get to the bottom of this ghastly affair soon enough. Everything will be all right. I promise."

CHAPTER 27

*G*inger helped Felicia dress in a respectable suit comprising a plaid skirt and long jacket over a complementary gold-coloured satin blouse. Ambrosia, having been summoned by Ginger, arrived all aflutter, looking like a large yellow melon in her saffron night dress and matching sleeping hat.

"Ginger! You *must* put a stop to this! This is outrageous! Reprehensible! The Gold name shall never recover!"

The dowager's soft face flushed deep red, and Ginger worried the elderly woman would have an apoplectic attack. "I'm afraid it's out of my hands, Grandmother. But you must calm yourself."

"Calm myself? *Calm* myself!"

Langley hovered nervously at the door. "Please get Lady Gold some tea," Ginger said.

Boss, sensing the emotional excitement, transferred himself from the comfort of his bed in Ginger's room to Felicia's and sat in the middle of the floor where he could view everyone, his big brown eyes scanning the room.

"Should I pack a bag?" Felicia said as if she was on her way to stay at a friend's house rather than spending the night in a jail cell.

Ginger regarded her with compassion the weight of a boulder. She felt crushed by her love for Felicia and her own helplessness in stopping this charade.

"You won't need a bag, love."

Felicia nodded her understanding and glanced despondently at the floor.

Ambrosia had claimed one of the two pink satin chairs positioned near the end of the bed, and Langley, with surprising speed, returned with the tea.

"Let's all have a cup before we go," Ginger said. She didn't care how long Basil was left waiting.

Felicia took the chair beside Ambrosia, and Ginger sat on the ottoman at the foot of the bed.

"What's going to happen to me?" Felicia asked quietly. The energetic confidence that usually laced her voice had disappeared.

Boss whimpered and strutted to Felicia's side. She patted her leg indicating permission to jump up and Boss landed lightly in her lap. Boss was devoted to Ginger but he was a sensitive little fellow, intuitive to the one most needing his comfort. Felicia burrowed her face into his soft fur.

"They'll . . . charge you," Ginger answered carefully. "And you'll spend the night in a cell."

"Oh good Lord!" Ambrosia sputtered. "How utterly ridiculous. We'll never live it down. I shan't be able to walk the streets of Chesterton again, much less go to church. The gossip!"

"Grandmother," Ginger said through pursed lips. "Now's hardly the time to worry about what other people think. Felicia is in trouble."

Ambrosia's heavy lids blinked and she let out a long sigh. "Of course, you're right." She reached for Felicia's hand. "It's just that I love you so, child. I can't bear this and it just comes out all wrong."

"I understand, Grandmama," Felicia said. "I love you, too."

"I promise you both that I'll do everything in my power to clear Felicia's name and get a prompt release," Ginger said.

A tear trickled down Felicia's face. "Ginger, you are the best sister a girl could ask for."

Ginger's heart almost burst. "We three Gold women—we are all in this together."

They finished their tea and Ambrosia hugged Felicia on the landing. "I can't bear to look at that awful man," she said, referring to Basil. Ginger felt the same way, though she knew she was being unreasonable. *Inspector* Reed was simply doing his job.

The fact didn't make her heart ache less.

Felicia stood tall as she walked down the staircase, but her nerves gave out on seeing Basil in the entrance hall waiting for her. She leaned into Ginger for support.

"It's going to be all right, love," Ginger said, holding her close. "It's going to be all right."

The next day Haley arrived, wearing her traditional tweed suit with a small suitcase in hand.

Seeing her friend when she needed her so, made the back of Ginger's eyes burn with emotion. This in itself perturbed Ginger. Usually, she remained stoic when confronted with danger or stress. Felicia's plight moved her in ways those other oft-dangerous situations had not. Faced with losing Felicia had stirred her feelings of loss for Daniel all over again.

Haley stared at Ginger with wide-eyed consternation. "Honey, whatever is the matter?"

"Have you heard? Is that why you've come?"

"Heard what?" Haley set her suitcase down in the entrance hall and removed her coat and scarf. She handed them to Wilson who then discreetly left the two friends alone.

"About Felicia's arrest."

Haley pivoted on her low Oxford heel. "*What?* I hadn't heard about that. I'm here because of the inquest tomorrow."

With all that had happened in the last twenty-four hours, Ginger had forgotten about the inquest. The knot in her stomach tightened. The inquest could go either way. Cast doubt on Felicia as a suspect, or add another nail to her coffin. They reached the sitting room and she flopped into the nearest chair.

"It's been simply dreadful."

Haley sat on the edge of the seat beside Ginger and leaned in. "I'm a mass of curiosity. What happened?"

Ginger relayed the events of the day previous, the interviews, the fracas with Smithwick and finally the analysis report on the knitting needle.

"Leaving her at the station like a criminal shredded me to bits," Ginger said. She found it hard to forgive Basil's part in it and had refused his offer for a lift home. Instead, she'd asked Constable Ryan to do it. "The whole matter is simply horrid."

Haley shook her head, dark curls escaping her faux bob. "Unbelievable. Surely, after getting to know Felicia, Inspector Reed can't seriously think her capable of such a horrendous crime."

"Exactly!"

"But, to be fair," Haley added reluctantly. "Felicia hadn't been presenting her best side over the weekend. And, an inspector worth his own weight would never let his personal feelings sway how he handled a case."

Ginger harrumphed. Haley was right, of course, but Ginger couldn't help but feel slighted. She was sure the inspector had shown feelings for her beyond ordinary proper protocol. Had she read the signals wrong? Then again, he did tend to blow hot and cold.

And so did she. Subconsciously she'd known of the cycle she'd fallen into with Basil, one of flirtation and restraint. They were bad for each other that way. And why should she care about an indefinable relationship with this man, when her heart still belonged to another?

Basil's job might be his priority, but family was hers.

"It makes me sick knowing that Felicia is sitting in a jail cell as we speak," she said. Her mind went to Daniel. She silently asked for forgiveness for failing to take proper care of his sister.

Haley poured coffee from the vacuum flask on the sideboard. Since Ginger's arrival, coffee had been set out and it and the tea were regularly topped up.

"And here I had you and the good inspector pegged to be together," she said.

Ginger groaned with exasperation. "Haley, dearest. I can promise you that scenario will *never* happen."

Haley paused with her coffee cup midway to her mouth as her wide jaw fell open. "Wow, you *are* angry."

Ginger stated simply, "I'm furious."

"Where is Inspector Reed, anyway?" Haley said. "It must be mighty awkward with him staying here."

"He's left. Took a room at the Chesterton Inn."

"I see," Haley said after a sip. "That's for the best, then."

"Indeed."

CHAPTER 28

*G*inger and Haley arrived at the police station the next morning to see Felicia. Ginger scanned the station searching for Basil Reed and hoped against hope that she wouldn't see his face.

Haley nudged her with her elbow and whispered, "He's not here."

Ginger clung to Haley's arm and whispered back, "I'm so glad you came."

"Me too, honey," Haley said warmly. Ginger found her friend's Boston accent calming. Haley's speech was always slow and relaxed, lazy around the consonants, soft like a lullaby. The quick, crisp and sometimes indecipherable accents of the English sounded extraordinarily sharp to Ginger's ears in tense times such as these.

Constable Ryan manned the front desk and

Ginger approached. He, at least, had the decency to look sheepish.

"Lady Gold and Miss Higgins here to visit Miss Felicia Gold," Ginger stated matter-of-factly.

"Yes, madam," The young constable squirmed behind the desk, his ruddy cheeks growing red. "We don't generally allow more dan one visitor at a time, madam, unless t'person is accompanied by a solicitor."

Ginger pierced him with a green-eyed glare. "I don't think you need to abide by that rule in this instance. We're not going to help her escape."

"Right, um, yes, well, since it's you, I'm sure it's fine."

The constable opened a drawer and removed a large iron ring that had a number of dangling keys and opened the jail cell.

Felicia's eyes were red and her flawless skin blotchy.

"Ginger!" She wiped away a stray tear with a well-manicured fingernail. Pearl polish, Ginger noted. The same one used to paint the knobs of the knitting needles.

Ginger removed her gloves and took Felicia's hands—they were cold and damp—and held them tightly in her own. "How are you holding up?" she asked.

Felicia trembled yet stood tall. "I'm all right, all things considered."

Releasing Ginger's hands, Felicia reached for Haley's. "So good to see you, Miss Higgins. Thank you for coming."

"We'll do whatever we can, to help," Haley said.

"I've called my solicitor in London," Ginger said. "And he's recommended the very best defence solicitor in England. I will meet with him after the inquest." She stared deeply into Felicia's eyes. "You'll be cleared and free in no time."

Felicia collapsed onto the hard wooden bench. "Oh, I do hope you're right."

Ginger sat alongside her. "I am right. This is all a terrible, terrible mistake." Ginger thought of Basil Reed and how embarrassed he'd be when he was proved wrong.

"Has anyone else been to see you?" Ginger asked. She didn't want to say Smithwick's name aloud, but Felicia's eyes registered understanding.

"No. No one."

"Are they treating you well here?"

"Well enough I suppose," Felicia said, listlessly. "The food is edible."

"Did you sleep okay?"

"Not really."

Ginger was worried about Felicia's lethargy. The torpid edge to her voice. Her normal spirited self had been cut off at the knees by this mess. Already Ginger missed her sister-in-law's feistiness. This sense of brokenness scared her.

"We're off to the inquest," Ginger said, keeping her voice strong. "We just wanted to make sure you were all right."

"I'm fine, Ginger. I really don't want you to worry so much about me."

Ginger would worry, but she wouldn't sit around and do nothing. The inquest was sure to provide answers. Then this nightmare would be over.

The village of Chesterton didn't have a crown court, so the inquest was held at the Chesterton Inn. Ginger assumed she'd see Basil there but she didn't expect to run into him, *literally*.

Ginger and Haley were entering the large gathering room at the back of the inn, just as Basil was stepping out, and for a short uncomfortable moment, they were standing nose to nose. The bruising on Basil's face had somehow made him even more appealing and the scent of his cologne...

"Lady Gold," Basil said with surprise. "I beg your pardon."

Ginger stepped back sharply. "Of course."

"You look well," he said.

Despite her indignation, her heart twittered in his presence—a visceral response that vexed her. What was the matter with her? She wasn't a young, impressionable girl, but a grown, sensible woman. She responded coolly. "If you wouldn't mind moving aside so we can pass."

Basil's eyes filled with regret. "I take it you're still cross at me."

Ginger scowled.

Haley answered for her. "Just a bit."

Basil tipped his hat towards Haley. "Hello, Miss Higgins." He then stepped around them and made his way down the hallway. Ginger watched him as he went. Though he walked tall, he limped slightly, favouring his left side. Ginger let out a breath. She *was* angry but quite honestly, she could say her anger was no longer directed at Basil. She was angry at the circumstances, which he represented.

Haley took her arm. "Now that we've got that over with, let's go in."

The room was finished entirely in stained mahogany. A makeshift jury's station and witness stand had been set up, and chairs arranged in a semi-circle around them. Teeming with people, it was nearing standing room only, and Ginger wondered if all of Chesterton had come out for the show. She doubted the village had seen so much excitement since the war.

Places were reserved for witnesses in the front row and Ginger and Haley shuffled past the spectators to claim two empty seats. Ginger felt the eyes of the villagers watching them, and she entertained a spot of vanity, feeling glad she'd chosen to wear an original

Parisian-designed burgundy straw hat with curlicues that covered the top and spilled over to one side.

Low muttering reached her ears.

"That's the killer's sister-in-law."

"Heard it were Miss Gold that done it."

"Don't that put the dowager in her place?"

"Pompous hat."

Haley whispered in Ginger's ear. "Ignore them."

Dr. Guthrie sat in a disgruntled heap at the end of the row. His white hair sprung from his head as if the man had been electrocuted. His eyes were closed, his pointy chin bearing down, and he emitted a soft snore. Ginger and Haley shuffled past his bony knees, rousing the man who startled with a loud snort.

"Hello, Dr. Guthrie," Haley said as she sat beside him.

"Oh, it's you."

Haley grinned. "That's what I love about you, Dr. Guthrie. So cheery."

Her playfulness garnered her a grunt.

The coroner, a short, well-fed man, called the room to order and began the proceedings.

"Please remember that no one is on trial here today. The purpose of this inquest is to establish the identity of the deceased, the place and time of death, and to determine how the deceased came by her death."

The jury, a collection of citizens from the surrounding areas of Hertfordshire, viewed pictures of the body provided by both the police and the pathologist.

The first witness to be called was the victim's sister, Mrs. Cecil Dunsbury. She wore a conservative day dress with a finely pleated calf-length skirt. Her hair, recently styled with perfect finger curls, framed her face. Though she stood gracefully upright, the twitching muscles around her mouth betrayed her nerves. The coroner asked her to give evidence to the identity.

"That is my sister in those pictures," she said softly. She took a moment to dab at teary eyes with a cotton handkerchief. "I also viewed the body at the mortuary."

Next the coroner called Clement, the gardener who'd found the body, who resided at 31 Racket Street in Chesterton.

"I was cleanin' up the garden near the lake behind Bray Manor. The fog was real low, crawlin' through the valley like it does this time of year. I was sweepin' dried up leaves off the veranda where they'd been blown overnight when from the corner of me eye I sees this dark form on the grass by the lake. At first I thought it was a lap rug or coat just thrown down, but then I sees a bit of white what looked like skin. I walks to the water at the edge of the lake like, and when I saw it was a girl, I ran to the back doors of Bray Manor, yellin' fer 'elp."

"And that's when Lady Gold and her guest Miss Higgins entered the scene?"

"Yes, sir. That's right."

"Did you touch the body, Mr. Clement, or in any way interfere with the scene?"

"No, sir. I'd don't mind cleanin' up a garden, but when it comes to dead things bigger than a insect, me stomach can't take it."

The coroner released the gardener and called on Ginger to give evidence. Slipping awkwardly past Dr. Guthrie's knees, Ginger walked with all the dignity she could muster, her head high, her eyes alight with fight. Standing behind the witness stand, she scanned the room in defiance, holding Basil's gaze for longer than she should have.

"Lady Gold," the coroner said. "You were second on the scene, is that correct?"

"Yes, sir. Along with Miss Higgins, my guest at Bray Manor."

"Please tell us your experience on the morning of the twenty-eighth of October."

"Miss Higgins and I were having breakfast in the morning room when my dog Boss began to bark. He noticed a man in distress outside the French windows and called attention to his plight." Ginger smiled at the jury. "He *really* is a clever dog."

"Thank you, Lady Gold." The coroner said, not looking a bit interested in the canine's intelligence quotient. "What happened next?"

"Mr. Clement pointed out the body, and I ran to see who it was." Ginger's heart squeezed at the memory of that short moment when she'd feared the woman on the grass was Felicia.

"Did you touch the body, Lady Gold?"

"The body was facedown. I rolled it onto its side to see the face. Then I let it roll back to the position I found it in."

"What happened next?"

"The police were called."

"How long until they arrived?"

"My guess is twenty minutes."

"And what did you do in this time?"

"Do? Nothing. We waited. It was traumatic for us all."

"At what point was the decision made to call the medical examiner?"

"Miss Higgins noticed a wound on Miss Ashton's back." Ginger added proudly, "She's training to be a doctor. At first, it just looked like another spot of mud."

Haley was called on next to confirm Ginger's evidence. "As a nurse," the coroner said, "were you able to determine the nature of the injury?"

"Only that there was a puncture wound. I thought it might be a bullet wound based on the diameter."

Sergeant Maskell was next to provide testimony.

"The telephone rang, a call from Bray Manor at nine minutes past eight the morning of the twenty-eighth." He spoke to the jury. "There's a big clock on the wall by the phone, a new electric one, so it don't run out of battery, and I looked at it when the report came in—that's how I know the exact time."

"By your account, what time did you arrive at the scene?"

"About twenty minutes later. That's how long it normally takes, and the roads were muddy that morning from the rain. In fact, I remembered to check my wristwatch and it was half past eight on the nose."

"And what did you find when you got there?"

"The butler, what's his name?" He hesitated. "Oh, yes, Wilson, showed us—me and Constable Ryan, that is—to Livingston Lake at the back of the manor. I knew we'd been called there because of a body, they said that much over the telephone, so I searched the ground and spotted something lying half in the water not far from the jetty."

"Who else was present at the scene?"

"Besides myself and Constable Ryan, Lady Gold, Miss Higgins and the butler."

"At what point did you determine the medical examiner should be called?"

"Well, at first I figured the young lady had possibly drunk too much at the dance and wandered onto the jetty only to fall in and drown. When the injury on the back was pointed out by Miss Higgins, I concluded the poor woman's death could be the result of foul play."

"Was it your decision to involve Scotland Yard?"

Sergeant Maskell paused as if he wanted to claim responsibility but not enough to perjure himself. "No, it was not."

"Whose was it, then?"

"It was Lady Gold's idea, sir."

Ginger scoffed inwardly, rueing the fact she'd suggested they asked for Inspector Reed specifically. However, she had to concede, the end result would as likely have been the same, and Basil did treat Felicia with more respect than another inspector might have.

Oh, her emotions! She really wanted to be cross with Basil Reed.

Haley poked Dr. Guthrie in the ribs when the coroner called on him to come forward.

The coroner instructed, "Please state your name and official capacity." Ginger wondered if the coroner was testing the man's mental state.

Now that he was on the stand, Dr. Guthrie came alive, speaking with the authority given to him by the county. "Dr. Peter Guthrie, medical examiner and police surgeon for the village of Chesterton and outlying areas such as the property known as Bray Manor."

"Please give your evidence."

"I arrived to find the deceased behind the residence

known as Bray Manor. She was face down on the grass bordering Livingston Lake, the lower half of the torso submerged. After ascertaining that the woman's life was indeed extinguished, I had the body transported to the mortuary where I performed a post mortem."

"Please relay the results of your examination."

"The absence of water in the lungs rules out drowning, pointing to the victim either being thrown, or falling into the water after death."

"Were there any indicators in the stomach contents?"

"A good amount of champagne, but no poisons of any kind."

"Were you able to determine the time of death?"

"There are many factors involved in narrowing down the window of time during which a deceased person's life was extinguished. Body temperature is a useful factor, but given the corpse was cooled by the lake and the exterior temperature being as low as it was, the time of death must be ascertained in other ways. According to Sergeant Maskell, the victim was last seen alive after the dance, at midnight. Rigor mortis was in the rigid state, and lividity was set. Therefore my estimate for time of death is between midnight and five in the morning."

"And the cause of death?"

"A foreign object piercing the heart."

"And what is the object?"

"I'm unable to say conclusively."

"Not a bullet wound?"

"No. There was no exit wound nor a bullet lodged in the body."

"I see. Can you say with all certainty that the injury wasn't accidental or self-inflicted?"

"I can."

"Is it possible a knitting needle could produce this type of injury and inflict deadly harm?"

"Yes, it is."

"That is all, Dr. Guthrie."

The coroner appeared satisfied with the evidence presented, and after an appeal to the jury, gave his verdict: wilful murder by a person or persons unknown.

CHAPTER 29

*A*mbrosia was in a horrible funk when Ginger and Haley returned from the inquest. They had barely got inside before the older woman assaulted them, bejewelled fingers slicing the air.

"What happened? Are they going to let Felicia go?"

"It wasn't a trial, Grandmother," Ginger said. "It was an inquest to determine the nature of death."

"Were there very many people there? Oh goodness, how the tongues must be wagging. I'll never be able to show my face again. My granddaughter arrested, and everyone knowing it. For murder no less!"

Other tongues might be flapping but Ginger bit hers. Ambrosia's fears for Felicia only manifested as concern about what people would think about her.

The dowager, Ginger reminded herself, was still decidedly entrenched in high society propriety.

"You must remain calm, Grandmother. For Felicia's sake. I promise we'll get to the bottom of this, and Felicia will return home to us."

"But the damage has already been done. She'll never find a suitable husband now."

The rapid tapping of Ambrosia's walking stick accompanied her out of the room.

"She's a force to be reckoned with, isn't she?" Haley muttered.

Ginger nodded. "Quite."

They agreed to meet in the sitting room after taking time to change their clothes. Ginger, the first to return, imagined Haley had started reading and got lost in one of her medical books like she often did. Phyllis made some fresh tea, and Ginger poured herself a cup. Teacup and saucer in hand, Ginger meandered to the window and stared at the lake. She tried to imagine Angela Ashton's last moments. Leaving the dance, wandering to the jetty in a clumsy, tipsy fashion. *Were you alone? Or was someone with you?*

Angela had fallen off near the end of the jetty. Was it before or after she'd been stabbed? Must've been after, Ginger thought, or the killer would've got wet, soaked enough that someone might've noticed later. Why was only half of Angela's body in the water? If she'd fallen off the jetty, even at the end near the edge, she would've fallen perpendicular to the water line. If not completely immersed, at least the whole length of the body would be soaked. The waves on Livingston Lake weren't like ocean waves, more like strong ripples. There wasn't a current, and even during a heavy storm, the wind wasn't energetic enough to push a body halfway onto the grass.

Did someone pull her out? But why risk getting caught? Again, a lake wouldn't drag a body into itself. She remembered how she and Haley had tried to re-enact the crime. On the jetty or on the grass, how had a stabbing landed Angela only halfway into the lake?

A flash of black ran across the green of the lawn, and Ginger smiled. Wilson was throwing a stick for Boss to catch. So, Ginger thought with a grin, Wilson wasn't the stuffy butler he liked people to think he was.

Though five years old, Boss's energy was like a pup. No matter how high or how far Wilson threw the stick, Boss caught it every time and ran it back to Wilson for another go.

She hadn't heard anyone come in and startled when Haley spoke.

"What are you looking at?"

"Don't sneak up on me like that!"

"I didn't sneak up." Haley joined her at the window.

"Boss and Wilson are playing fetch." Ginger watched as Wilson threw it, sometimes high, sometimes low, and sometimes straight on. She turned to Haley. "Do you recall the angle of the entry wound?"

"It was hard to tell at first glance because the wound had collapsed in on itself."

"Could you measure it conclusively?"

"If that was your intention, then yes."

Ginger's eyes flashed with intuition. "I think we need to pay Dr. Guthrie another visit."

Thankfully, Wilson had made sure that the mechanic had seen the Humber, so it was back in good service. Haley held a hand against the dash and another on the door handle as if that would keep the motorcar upright as Ginger darted around puddles and potholes.

"What if he's not at the surgery?" Haley asked loudly. "It is after four."

"Where else would he be?"

"Good point. Tell me again why we're searching for Dr. Guthrie?"

"Something's bothering me about his evidence."

"So you've said, but you've failed to say what."

"That's because I can't put my finger on it. Just something fussing in my brain."

Ginger had got directions from Phyllis. She'd remembered passing the small surgery on an earlier journey through Chesterton, and it was only a short distance from the Croft Convalescent Home.

After a quick enquiry at the reception and an assurance that Dr. Guthrie was still in, Ginger and Haley soon came upon the room where the corpse had been examined. Ginger knocked confidently on the door.

"Dr. Guthrie?"

When he didn't answer she pushed on the door and it swung open easily. Dr. Guthrie sat at his desk, head back, eyes closed and mouth slack.

A patch of red on his shirt. Ginger's pulse leapt. Had the man been attacked? "Dr. Guthrie!"

Shouting his name had the desired effect of snapping the doctor back to life.

"Wh-what? Good Lord!" The man frowned, the map lines on his face deepening. "Lady Gold. Miss Higgins. What is the meaning of this?"

"I'm so sorry, Dr. Guthrie," Ginger said. "I didn't mean to frighten you. When you didn't respond, and then I saw your shirt . . . I worried the worst had happened."

The doctor glanced at the splotch of red on his chest and harrumphed. "Blood. From the steak I just ate. I like 'em rare. And no, I don't bother eating at home when I have work to do. Now, why are you here?"

"We're wondering if you wouldn't mind allowing us a look at the body, Dr. Guthrie," Haley answered. "We're particularly curious about the angle of the wound."

Dr. Guthrie's eyes narrowed in consideration, he huffed, then nodded his head.

Not officially a mortuary, the room where the post mortem had been performed was painted white with a porcelain sink and ceramic counter and table tops.

Miss Ashton's body, grey as ash lay under a white surgery sheet, with only her head showing. Ginger sighed. She was such a beautiful girl with so much to live for. Such a shame.

The doctor rolled the corpse over. The injury on the back upper left side had been cleaned out and dried. "The stab wound is at a ninety-degree-angle." Dr. Guthrie opened a drawer and pulled out a file full of photographs taken during the post mortem. "You can see it here where it pierced the muscle tissue." Ginger grimaced. The photograph was from the inside of the chest cavity after the heart had been removed.

Dr. Guthrie provided another photo, this one of the heart. "A clean entry wound, clearly a ninety-degree penetration."

"What does that mean?" Ginger asked. "What is the significance?"

The doctor spun on his heel, so his back was to her. "Pretend to stab me."

Ginger tentatively laid a hand on the doctor's shoulder, as she imagined the killer would have done to Angela Ashton, and "stabbed" him with her other arm.

"How are you holding the weapon?"

Ginger closed a fist, palm up.

"That would make the most sense," Haley said. "The natural thing to do would be to raise your arm, like you did, and draw it down."

"But the stabbing didn't happen that way," Ginger said. "She 'stabbed' the doctor again, holding the imaginary weapon horizontally yet high enough to reach his heart. That doesn't feel natural," she said. "I can't imagine why someone would hold the weapon that way."

"Try it on me," Haley said. "I'm closer to the victim's height."

"Ginger went through the motion and again was struck by the awkwardness of the movement. It's difficult to insert it straight on," she said. "The most natural way is to angle down with a hard thrust. An upward thrust could work, too."

"I concur with your conclusions," Dr. Guthrie said.

"So how did it happen?" Ginger asked. "Are we wrong about the knitting needle?" The blood traces were small, but they were *there*.

The doctor made a slight sideways motion with his head. "I don't think so, Lady Gold."

Ginger imagined the scenario again with the stabbing straight on, and her eyes grew wide.

"I think I know what happened."

CHAPTER 30

Ginger raced through Chesterton with only two cars honking at her, which she thought promising.

Haley, on the other hand, yelled out several times. "We won't solve this murder if you get us killed first!"

With Haley on her heels, Ginger dramatically entered the police station, the fringe of her Scottish hand-painted scarf streaming behind in her wake.

Constable Ryan jumped to attention when he saw her. "Lady Gold?"

She adjusted her wide-brimmed hat. "I need to see Inspector Reed. It's urgent!"

The constable ducked his chin. "I'm afraid he's left."

"What do you mean, he's left?"

"He's gone back to London."

Ginger froze at his words, the implications

piercing her heart. Basil had given up on Felicia. He had left without saying goodbye. He'd given up on *her*.

She swallowed hard. "How long has he been gone?"

"He left t'station—" Constable Ryan's eyes darted to the clock on the wall. "Twenty-five minutes ago."

Twenty-five minutes. He could still be at the inn.

She nearly sprinted to the door and shouted to Haley. "We have to catch him."

"What about Felicia?"

Ginger stuttered to a stop. Felicia was still at the station waiting for Ginger to return from the inquest, which had ended over two hours ago. She looked at Haley. "Can you—?"

Haley waved her off. "Of course. Go!"

There were only a few motorcars in the parking area in front of the Chesterton Inn and in fact, more horses and carts were parked along the street than automobiles. Ginger quickly scoured the area for a forest-green Austin 7.

Her heart sank. It wasn't there. If Basil had left for London, reaching him by telephone might take two or more hours.

The killer could kill again.

For once, Ginger was thankful that Felicia was locked up at the police station. There at least she would be safe.

Ginger turned the Humber around and saw

Basil's Austin parked across the road. She parked behind it and walked swiftly to the Inn.

"Is Inspector Reed in?" she said to the clerk behind the front desk.

The clerk checked his calendar. "I've only just started my shift, madam. Let me see."

His movements were slow and methodical, and it was all Ginger could do to snatch the book and read it for herself.

"Ah, there it is," the clerk said. "It looks like he's checked out."

"But his car is across the road."

"Perhaps he's gone somewhere on foot."

That must be the case. She headed out trying to guess where Basil could've possibly gone, when she spotted him leaning up against his motorcar, arms folded over his chest, watching her.

Ginger slowed, her mouth growing dry at the sight of him. She admired a fine dresser, but Basil was more than that. He was confident and self-assured, yet his eyes betrayed a weakness. Ginger perceived it was the modicum of concern and yes, desire, he had for her. She couldn't deny that they shared a connection beyond what mere colleagues experience, a tight rope neither of them, apparently, was willing to traverse. Yet, he would've left without another word to her, had she not sought him out first.

"Are you looking for me?" Basil said as she approached.

Normally, Ginger would've responded coyly, engaged him in harmless, verbal sparring, but there was too much on the line right now.

"I know who killed Miss Ashton."

Basil agreed that an impromptu meeting of the knitting circle was in order and within two hours, everyone was summoned and was in the sitting room at Bray Manor. Ginger asked Wilson to join them and to guard the door. Boss sat near the butler's feet as if he understood the urgency and wanted to help.

Mrs. Richards, on one side of Ambrosia, wore a thick, knitted cardigan, no doubt one of her own creations; the Honourable Mrs. Croft, slumped in the high-back chair next to Mrs. Richards looked taller than she was due to her long torso, and she slouched to make up for it.

Miss Smith took the chair closest to the fireplace. A large handbag, big enough to hold several books, was on the floor beside her feet which were shod with shoes as sensible as Haley's; and Miss Whitton was in her nurse's uniform with her name tag, Sister Whitton, still attached. Haley sat beside the nurse on the settee.

"I don't understand what this is all about," Mrs. Richards said with much agitation. "I'm missing my bridge club."

The Honourable Mrs. Croft looked frightened.

Uncharacteristically, she kept her head bowed and gaze diverted. Miss Smith sat like a perky lap dog, unperturbed. To her, any excitement was better than none at all.

Miss Whitton slumped in a chair and yawned into her palm. "I had a long shift today," she said. "I hope this meeting won't be long."

With the flickering shadows cast by the roaring fire, you could almost miss the bruising on Inspector Reed's face, but Miss Whitton's sharp eye spotted it. "What happened to you, Inspector?"

"Just a minor accident," he said quickly. "Nothing to worry about. But my jaw is tender, so I hope you ladies won't mind if Lady Gold speaks on my behalf."

Ginger looked to Basil, and he nodded for her to begin.

"I'm sure you're all wondering why you've been called here, and I'll tell you straightaway. Miss Ashton was stabbed to death with Miss Gold's knitting needle, which went missing at the last knitting association meeting. I'm happy to make the pronouncement that Miss Gold has been released and all charges dropped. She is now resting."

Gasps filled the room followed by protestations.

Miss Whitton: I assumed it was something like that.

Mrs. Richards: Surely, you don't suspect any of us?

Miss Smith: Anyone could've taken it. A servant, perhaps, or even a guest from the ball.

Ambrosia: It was the poltergeist. I've heard they turn nasty after a while.

"Ladies!" Ginger clapped her palms together. "Please calm down."

The eruption of voices silenced, and Ginger continued. "Let's first address the matter of the poltergeist."

"You don't actually believe a ghost killed her, do you?" asked Miss Whitton with a look of contempt.

"I definitely don't. In fact, we've already had a confession. It's been dealt with and we don't need to mention it." Ginger hoped to preserve the Honourable Mrs. Croft's dignity, but the woman herself felt compelled to confess and burst into tears.

"I'm sorry, Dowager Lady Gold! I don't know what got into me."

Ambrosia looked as if she'd choked on a fishbone. Her face flushed at the offence, and then with shame at her gullibility. "*Mrs. Croft!*"

"I know, I know. Please do forgive me," Mrs. Croft said, her voice in near hysterics. "I can't go to prison!"

Ambrosia stilled. "No don't be silly. No one goes to prison for playing a practical joke."

Though she'd be a social outcast, Ginger thought, if word got out. "Let us commit to keeping mum about Mrs. Croft's confession," she said. "A knitting circle secret."

Ambrosia's large eyes grew round with an alternative possibility. "Unless——"

"No!" Mrs. Croft snapped. "I didn't kill Miss Ashton." She appealed to the room. "*I didn't!*"

"Please calm yourself, Mrs. Croft," Ginger said. "We know you didn't kill Miss Ashton."

"You do?" Her eyelashes batted as relief at her proclaimed innocence took effect. "Then who did?'"

Ginger stood as she answered. "The killer knew you were the poltergeist and saw you take Miss Gold's knitting needle. An opportunity presented itself—two actually. The first was when Mrs. Croft turned her back on her knitting basket, making way for another to snatch it, and the second was the dance, where the killer knew the victim was going to be in attendance."

Ginger took in each eager face as she addressed the room.

"Every one of you here, apart from myself and Miss Higgins, the inspector, Dowager Lady Gold, and Wilson, had motive. Yours Mrs. Croft was obvious— you didn't want your son to follow through on his promise to wed Miss Ashton. That was widely known."

"But, you said . . ."

Ginger held up a palm. "Miss Whitton, like all of Chesterton, knew that Miss Ashton behaved unbecomingly towards her younger brother, James, and wanted to preserve his reputation and his future. She wasn't seen at the dance, but that doesn't mean she couldn't have waited outside."

Miss Whitton pressed firm lips before spouting, "I was at home with my brother."

"Of course," Ginger said.

"Mrs. Richards lost a beloved pet due to Miss Ashton's carelessness."

"Yes, I blamed her for Pal's death," Mrs. Richards said defensively as she pushed her thick spectacles to the bridge of her nose. "But, I can barely see to knit much less sneak up on someone in the dark."

"Yes, but this attack didn't require the ability to sneak up or exhibit physical strength because the weapon, the knitting needle, was catapulted."

Ambrosia's brow collapsed in confusion. "Whatever do you mean?"

Ginger locked eyes with the librarian. "I think you know, don't you Miss Smith."

Mary Smith's countenance turned to stone. "I don't think I do."

"Weren't you the one who brought up the archery association at the last meeting?"

"I can't recall."

"Don't you play with handmade archery sets to break the monotony of your time at Chesterton Library?"

Miss Smith folded her arms across her chest. "So what if I do?"

"When the inspector and I visited you at the library, you dropped a book into a desk drawer, and I confess I had a peek inside. At first, I didn't know what I was looking at, it only appeared to be evidence of one fooling with the pencils and elastic bands in one's desk."

"Like you said," Miss Smith said stiffly, "it's something I do to pass the time."

"You're a good archer, aren't you Miss Smith?" Ginger pressed. "A member of the archery club, I believe. You'd have no problem substituting a knitting needle for an arrow. It was you who killed Miss Ashton, wasn't it?"

CHAPTER 31

*I*t only took a split second for Miss Smith to swoop an arm towards the fire and pluck out a piece of wood that burned like a torch on one end. She swung the fire as if she were a wild caveman holding back the lions. The flames from the torch reflected in her spectacles, making her appear possessed.

"Stay back!" Miss Smith's voice went up an octave, her words like the screeching noise of nails on a blackboard. The hairs on Ginger's neck stood on end. "Easy, Miss Smith," she said calmly. "No one wants to hurt you."

"Liar!" Flames danced through the air as she shouted. "You want me to hang!"

"That's not true," Ginger said. "We want to help you."

"You're all liars and killers! With your silence."

Tears streamed down Miss Smith's face and a collective gasp rose when she almost lost control of the torch.

Miss Smith stared at each one in the room her voice steadying eerily. "All the citizens of Chesterton are guilty. My dear sister died and justice was not served."

Realization dawned. "Jean Smith was your sister?" Jean Smith was the fourth girl in the group that had worked on the sheep farm with Felicia.

Tears ran in rivulets down Mary Smith's face. "My only sister, ten years my junior. I raised her like my own when our mother died. She was the world to me."

A small sob escaped her lips, and Ginger felt a deep pang of empathy for the woman.

She pointed to Mrs. Richards. "Your husband was on the jury."

"Th-there were twelve of them," Mrs. Richard's sputtered. "Mr. Richards wasn't the only one."

"The jury was unanimous—which means they found those land girls innocent!"

"I'm sorry, Miss Smith," Miss Whitton said with her gentle nursing voice. "Your sister committed suicide."

"She was bullied into it!" Miss Smith screeched. "She was too plain pudding for them, and they made her life miserable! Angela Ashton was the worst of the lot. Always belittling her, telling Jean— my beautiful and gentle sister—that she was useless and ugly. The other girls did nothing to stop her. *They* killed my sister."

"Mary," Ginger started.

"Stop!" Mary Smith thrust out a palm. "Angela deserved to die. She was evil to the core. Always leading people on and then dropping them when it suited her. She was a loose and immoral woman who was destined to be a Baroness. She didn't deserve a life of privilege like that."

She stared hard at Ginger. "Felicia and Muriel Webb were to be next. I'll never forgive you for stopping me."

At this, Mary Smith made a large figure of eight with the burning wood, purposefully hitting the lace curtains.

"Miss Smith!" Basil barked, but it was too late. The curtains caught fire, the flames jumping from one panel to the next. Haley rushed to the sideboard for the jug of water, but it was too little too late.

Miss Whitton whipped at the flames with a knitted blanket, but it only stirred them and caused the afghan to catch fire as well.

"Everybody outside!" Ginger yelled. Miss Smith was ahead of the bunch, having snatched her handbag and escaped out of the French windows. Ginger hiked up her skirt and ran after her.

"Mary!"

The librarian was spry on her feet. The early

November night was cloudless and though the moon was only half-full, it shed enough light to see dimly. Mary Smith dropped her torch onto the dry grass, and Ginger lost valuable time stomping out the flames and throwing dirt on it until it was fully extinguished. Mary raced through the garden, but she didn't know the layout like Ginger did. She ran around the rose-bushes, through the begonias and behind the sycamore tree. Ginger felt the stinging bites of thorns and dry branches as they tore her skin, but her adrenaline pushed her onward.

Miss Smith had tried to throw Ginger off by circling back—a plan that backfired because she soon found herself cornered between the lake and the boathouse.

"Stay back," she threatened.

Ginger slowed, panting to gain her breath. When she looked up, Miss Smith had a bow and arrow pointing at Ginger's heart. The instrument was smaller than most, child-size, and fitting for the diminutive librarian. That was what she had stored away in her large handbag.

Ginger sprung behind the thick trunk of a maple tree and cringed at the sound of the first arrow penetrating the bark with a snap.

"I have a dozen arrows on me, Lady Gold, and as you know, I'm a good shot. You'd be wise to let me go."

"I can't do that Mary. You've killed a woman."

"And now *I* have to pay? Do you think I haven't already paid? My heart is broken . . ." Mary's voice cracked and large tears streamed down her face. "Jean wasn't pretty like the others. Nor rich or even that clever, but she was lovely, kind, and would never hurt a soul."

Ginger sighed. So much heartache in the world.

"I'm sorry for your loss," Ginger said. "I truly am. I know how it feels to needlessly lose someone dear."

Mary's eyes grew cold as the window of her emotional vulnerability closed. "It's not the same, Lady Gold. Sir Daniel died at the hands of the enemy. Jean died at the hands of her so-called *friends*."

The air had thickened with the tang of smoke, and Ginger's hand flew to her chest at the sight of the ridge of flames that licked at the darkening sky. Bray Manor was on *fire*. In the distance, the wail of sirens filled the air.

Ginger's attention was diverted for mere moments, but long enough for Mary to hop into the rowing boat. She scrambled for the oars.

Ginger jumped out from behind the tree. "Mary!"

The librarian swiftly lifted the bow and worked an arrow into place. She aimed it at Ginger. "Stay back."

Ginger darted back to the tree. Slipping her hand under the hem of her skirt, she reached for her garter and removed her Remington. She hated how much she'd been using the weapon lately.

She stepped out from the tree far enough to point. "Put the arrow down."

Mary let the arrow fly. Ginger backed up in the nick of time as it whizzed past her face. She stepped into position, revolver pointed. Mary hurried to load another arrow.

"I'll shoot you before you can fire it again."

Mary stared hard, tears streaming down her cheeks. "Go ahead! Kill me."

"I don't shoot to kill," Ginger said. "But it *will* hurt."

Mary Smith's shoulders dropped in defeat, letting the small bow fall to the floor of the boat.

"Ginger?"

Ginger didn't take her eyes off the librarian at the sound of Basil's voice and kept the pistol pointed should Mary get any wild ideas.

"Over here."

Basil broke through the bush. His eyes darted from Ginger and the pistol to the woman in the boat. Though his limp was intact, he strode with authority to the lake's edge.

"Miss Smith, I'm arresting you under the suspicion of the murder of Angela Ashton." He helped her out of the boat onto the jetty and placed cuffs on her wrists now behind her back. "You do not have to say anything but it may harm your defence if you do not mention, when questioned, something which you later rely on in court. Anything you do say may be given in evidence."

Ginger lowered the gun. It wasn't even loaded. She'd shot her last bullet when she'd broken up the fight between the inspector and the captain.

"How's Bray Manor?"

Basil's eyes flashed with regret. "Everyone is out and safe, but I'm afraid . . ."

Ginger didn't wait to hear the end of his sentence but took off like a shot through the darkness.

CHAPTER 32

*T*he Chesterton Inn emptied out considerably once the leaves fell—a lull before the Christmas visitors came through. Plenty of room for the Gold women and Haley to lodge temporarily.

Bray Manor had suffered considerable damage, the sitting room was gutted, and smoke damage was extensive throughout. The building was ancient and had been falling apart structurally over the years, and Ginger suspected it would cost much more to fix than one could ever sell it for.

Everyone was devastated by the loss, and tears were shed openly. Shattered by the fact that their livelihoods had literally gone up in flames, Bray Manor staff returned to their respective homes.

Since dinner had been missed, Haley insisted they

gather in the restaurant for a bite to eat. "We don't want anyone fainting from hunger."

Ginger paid the management well to close the restaurant for a private function—the four women needed time to share their grief together. When the fire started, Boss had run upstairs to Felicia's room to warn her of the danger. They considered him a hero, and Ginger ordered him his own piece of beef as a reward.

Though they mourned the loss of Bray Manor, Felicia's release from custody in Chesterton and the dropping of all charges was a reason to celebrate.

"It's good for us to eat and be thankful for what we do have. Family," Ginger said. Then squeezing Haley's hand, she added, "And friends."

Felicia ran fingers under her eyes. Ginger wasn't used to seeing Felicia without makeup, and her natural appearance made her look younger and more vulnerable than Ginger had ever seen her.

"Thank you for believing in me," Felicia said to her. "I'll never take my freedom for granted again."

"I've always believed in you." Tears leaked from Ginger's eyes at the gratitude she felt at the mended bridge between them.

Ambrosia fanned herself with a menu, her doughy cheeks flushed red with emotion. She wailed, "I can't believe my dear Bray Manor is gone!"

"It's my fault," Felicia said grimly. "It was my idea to bring strangers into the house."

"Nonsense," Ginger said. "Your ideas were innovative and would have been successful. You're not responsible for the actions of Miss Smith."

Felicia's eyes, brimmed once again with tears, pleaded, "But I knew how Angela treated Jean and I did nothing to stop it."

Ginger took Felicia's hand in hers and tenderly stroked it. "You were a child, Felicia, without the wisdom and hindsight of time. Sure you could've tried to stop Angela, but she might've just turned her venom on you. What happened to Jean Smith was tragic, but it wasn't your fault."

Felicia burst into tears and blew into her linen serviette in the most unladylike manner. "I'm sorry," she said. "It's just all so awful."

"Now, now, Felicia," Ambrosia said. "Do pull yourself together."

The older woman's lips quivered and Ginger sensed the admonition was for herself as well as her granddaughter.

Felicia let out a soft hiccup and hid the serviette under the table. "Yes, Grandmama."

"I agree with Ginger," Haley said. "Dr. Guthrie stated that Miss Jean Smith had known mental problems. Had she been given the help she needed, she might've stood up to Angela herself."

It was yet to be determined if Mary Smith was also plagued with mental problems. Perhaps, Ginger thought, a jury would show mercy and Mary's life would be spared

"Thank you, Miss Higgins," Felicia said. "I appreciate your saying so."

Haley inclined her head and smiled. "Would you find it possible to call me Haley? I know I'm a foreigner . . ." Her gaze moved to Ginger relating what was left unspoken. *And a commoner.*

"I'd love that," Felicia said, her eyes brightening a little. "And you must call me Felicia."

Ambrosia watched the exchange with an expression of incredulity. "I'll remain Dowager Lady Gold if that's all right with you."

"Of course, madam," Haley said, biting the inside of her lip to keep from smiling.

Ambrosia returned to her own woes. "Whatever are we going to do? We can't live in this inn forever."

"Not forever, Grandmama," Felicia said with a deep sigh. She'd lost her vivaciousness since her break from Captain Smithwick and her stint as a prisoner. Ginger hoped that time would heal the wounds of her sister-in-law's embarrassment and disillusionment. Captain Smithwick had disappeared from Chesterton and Ginger could only hope that he had gone for good.

"How do you know?" Ambrosia insisted. "Even though the north wing remains, the firemen said it suffered tremendous smoke damage." Her round eyes rolled upwards. "Oh, dear. I feel faint."

"Drink this," Ginger said, reaching over with a glass of water. "I'll order you some strong tea."

Ambrosia tilted the glass to her lips, stopping partway to continue with her grief. "And my poor staff —their jobs gone with the smoke."

Felicia patted her grandmother's hand. "It'll work out," she said dully. "I just need time to think it through."

Ginger shared a nervous smile with Haley. Earlier they'd discussed another possibility, and now Ginger made her final decision. "Grandmother and Felicia, you must come to Hartigan House and live with me."

The room stilled, both Felicia and Ambrosia froze momentarily until Felicia squealed. "Do you mean it, Ginger? Really?"

"Indeed," Ginger said, her smile broadening. "Hartigan House is certainly large enough for us all."

Ambrosia remained straight-faced. "What about my servants. I can't just abandon them."

Ginger shrugged. "Bring them too. I'm under-staffed right now anyway."

Except for a butler. Pips was irreplaceable.

Ambrosia addressed Ginger's unspoken concern. "Wilson was due to retire at the end of the month anyway, and Phyllis is getting married in the spring. Mrs. Beasley and Langley could come, I suppose. And Clement. Goodness knows Hartigan House is in need of a competent gardener."

"Great!" Ginger said. "Then it's settled."

The door to the restaurant opened, and a familiar voice rang out warmly, "I know this is a private function, but I hope you will let me say a few words before I go."

Ginger's gaze latched onto Basil. "Of course," she said civilly. "Come in."

Basil approached the table, hat in hand, and looked at Felicia. "I do want to apologise for the trouble I put you through, Miss Felicia."

Felicia's lips trembled, but she managed a small smile. "I understand that you were just doing your job, Inspector."

Ginger couldn't help but snort. She'd told Basil he was making a mistake when he arrested Felicia. That Felicia was innocent. Her sister-in-law's trauma could've been avoided.

Basil was insightful enough to pick up on how Ginger was feeling. "I hope that you can forgive me, Lady Gold, for not taking your word."

Ginger softened. It wasn't often that a man would admit publicly that he'd been wrong. And Ginger wasn't the type to hold a grudge. She sighed. "As Felicia has already said, you were simply doing your job."

Basil nodded and put his trilby hat back on his head. "I'll leave you now." His eyes settled on Ginger. "Please let me know if there is anything more you need."

The women remained silent until the inspector had gone.

Haley leaned into Ginger. "You're rather hard on him."

Ginger groaned inwardly. She was rather hard on herself. It was better this way. She and Basil weren't friends. Circumstances had put them in a close working relationship—that was all it was. Close quarters had simulated an intimacy that wasn't real. Besides, even though Basil had agreed to divorce his wife, Ginger knew that he was still in love with her.

And she was still in love with another, as well.

CHAPTER 33

*I*t took a few days before everything was settled. Ginger would drive Ambrosia to London in the Humber later that day, while Haley and Felicia along with Clement, Langley and Mrs. Beasley—who'd agreed to relocate—took the train. What they could salvage of their belongings would be shipped over later.

Ginger pulled the Humber to a halt in front of the Bray Manor ruins. It had been taped off to warn off looters and the curious; the grand blacken hall appeared starkly defeated against the grey sky.

She stepped out and walked around the charred remains to the lake behind. The damage to the house was worse from the back. The bricks darkened with soot, windows blown out with shattered glass on the ground beneath, the roof sunken and collapsing in parts. Ginger swallowed a lump, fighting against the emotion that had been building all morning, knowing what she had to do.

Ginger climbed into the rowing boat, gingerly settled onto the wooden seat at the back, and tucked the skirt of her black crepe de Chine dress under her legs. Lifting the oars, she carefully placed them into the water and rowed.

The paddles lapped gently through the waves and with each strong pull, the boat glided closer to her mark.

With each strong pull she glided closer to her grief.

It didn't fully hit her until she reached the small cemetery and located his grave. It was easy to spot—the gravestone was new and clean, and taller than the rest; the flowerbed in the foreground well-tended.

Felicia's charity.

Etched in delicate script were the words:

Sir Daniel Livingston Gold
7th April, 1895 - 2nd October , 1918
Loving son, grandson,
brother, and husband.

Ginger fell to her knees and freely wept. There was no one around to judge her, no one to stop her.

Until today, until *this*, it was easy to pretend that Daniel was just "away," to return someday. Now she had to face the facts; her Daniel was dead. He was never coming home.

She could still hear his voice in her head, warm as honey and gentle as a bubbling brook. *Someday, Ginger, this war will be over and we can settle down—Boston or London—you pick. Perhaps then the children will come.*

"I chose London, love," she whispered. There'd be no children. That was something she'd accepted long ago, even before Daniel had died.

Further down on the tombstone were these words of comfort:

"And God will wipe away all tears from their eyes; and there shall be no more death, neither sorrow nor crying nor pain; for the former things are passed away." Rev. 21:4

Behind her was the sound of a motorcar pulling into the entrance of the small graveyard. She frowned at the taxicab—who on earth? Then she recognised the passenger, a curly-haired brunette, wearing a tweed suit and sensible Oxford shoes. Ginger wiped her eyes as she watched Haley strolling towards her, Boss at her heels.

Neither of them spoke as Haley put a consoling arm around Ginger's shoulders and Boss whimpered at her feet. Ginger hadn't felt the cold until now. She scooped up her pet and held him close as she pressed into Haley's embrace. They stood there in silence.

"He was a very good man," Ginger finally said.

Haley hummed in agreement. "I wish I could've known him."

Ginger set Boss on the ground and watched him chase a squirrel as if he hadn't a care in the world. How she envied that. She crossed her arms over her chest as if the act itself could hold in the tidal wave of emotion that threatened to burst through.

"I'm so torn, Haley. I loved him very much—still love him, but I feel . . ."

"That it might be time to say goodbye?"

"Would that be awful?"

Ginger's normally perfectly coiffed hair fell over one eye and Haley gently pushed it behind Ginger's ear.

"Oh, honey. It's not awful. Daniel would want you to. He'd want you to be happy. You owe it to him to be happy."

"Because I lived?"

"Because you lived."

A greylag goose skidded across the south shore of Livingston lake, its orange beak disappearing under the slate-coloured surface as it nabbed its morning minnow. Joined by its mate, the two of them floated along squawking amiably as if they were discussing the news over breakfast tea.

Ginger's mind went to Basil Reed. Maybe it was time to put the picture of Daniel away.

"You've got awfully quiet," Haley said. "Are you all right?"

Ginger smiled softly. "Yes. I think I am."

The End.

ABOUT THE AUTHOR

Lee Strauss is the bestselling author of The Ginger Gold Mysteries series (cozy historical mystery), A Nursery Rhyme Suspense series (Mystery Sci-fi Romantic Suspense), The Perception series (young adult dystopian), and young adult historical fiction. When she's not writing or reading she likes to cycle, hike and kayak. She enjoys traveling (but not jet lag :0), cashew lattes, red wine and dark chocolate.

She also writes younger YA fantasy as Elle Strauss and sweet inspirational romance as Hope Franke Strauss.

For more info on books by Lee Strauss and her social media links visit leestraussbooks.com. To make sure you don't miss the next new release, be sure to sign up for her readers list!

If you enjoyed reading *Murder at Bray Manor* please help others enjoy it too.

- **Recommend it:** Help others find the book by recommending it to friends, readers' groups, discussion boards and by suggesting it to your local library.

- **Review it:** Please tell other readers why you liked this book by reviewing it at your point of purchase or Goodreads. If you do write a review, let me know at **leestraussbooks@gmail.com** so I can thank you.
- **Suggest it** to your local librarian.

This book has been edited and proofed, but typos are like little gremlins that like to sneak in when we're not looking. If you spot a typo, please report it to: **admin@laplumepress.com**

Stay tuned for news of the Ginger Gold Mystery Book 4 - *Murder at Feathers & Flair* by signing up for Lee's readers list

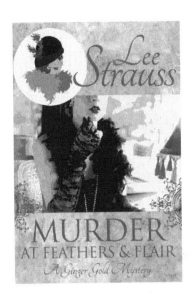

GINGER GOLD receives a letter from her sister-in-law, Felicia, requesting Ginger come straightaway to her late husband's family home, Bray Manor. Dowager Lady Gold, Ginger's nervous grandmother through marriage, believes the old manor is haunted.

Ginger doesn't believe in ghosts, but is haunted nevertheless by memories of her husband and the lure of his gravesite she just can't bring herself to visit.

In order to keep Bray Manor afloat financially, Felicia and Ambrosia have opened the estate to the public for club meetings and special events. Knitters, stamp collectors and gardeners converge weekly—targets for the zeitgeist that seems to find amusement in hiding small things from their owners.

Bray Manor hosts a dance to raise money for maimed soldiers who struggle with peacetime after the Great War. Felicia invites her flapper friends *and* her new beau, Captain Francis Smithwick, a man Ginger has met before and definitely doesn't like.

When the dance ends with the discovery of a body, Ambrosia is certain the poltergeist is to blame, but Ginger is quite sure the murderer is made of flesh and blood.

www.leestraussbooks.com

leestraussbooks@gmail.com

ACKNOWLEDGMENTS

Much love to the growing list of fans who love to hang out with Ginger Gold! You make writing these books a joy.

I couldn't do it without the help of my superhero team, Angelika Offenwanger, Robbi Bryant, Heather Belleguelle, and Shadi Bleiken. You guys rock!

As always, my heart belongs to my family—my husband Norm Strauss and kids, Joel, Levi, Jordan and Tasia. A special thanks and love shout out to my parents, Gene and Lucille Franke and my circle, Donna, Shawn, Noreen and Lori. I'm so grateful for your prayers and practical support.

Forever grateful to God who keeps me.